Two and two usually equalea

Yes, conc made

All the records had been there—the marriage of Danny's parents, the births of her siblings—all except Danny's.

Mitch could think of only one reason why her birth record wasn't there. For Danny's sake, though, he hoped he was wrong. He knew he had to approach the subject with her, but he dreaded it. He was in danger of losing his objectivity. If this were any other case, he wouldn't hesitate to tell the client what he'd found, what he suspected. He resisted telling Danny, not for professional reasons but for personal ones.

Get a grip on yourself, Mitch, he thought angrily. This is your job. No matter what you feel for her, you have an obligation to do the job she hired you to do.

Feel for her…?

Dear Reader,

What's a single FABULOUS FATHER to do when he discovers he has another daughter—a child he never knew about? Why, marry the secretive mom, of course! And that's exactly what he proposes in Moyra Tarling's *Twice a Father*. Don't miss this wonderful story.

This month, two authors celebrate the publication of their twenty-fifth Silhouette books! *A Handy Man To Have Around* is Elizabeth August's twenty-fifth book—and part of her bestselling miniseries, SMYTHESHIRE, MASSACHUSETTS. In this delightful novel, a tall, dark and gorgeous hunk sure proves to be A Handy Man To Have Around when a small-town gal needs big-time help!

Daddy on the Run is Carla Cassidy's twenty-fifth book for Silhouette—and part of her intriguing miniseries THE BAKER BROOD. In this heartwarming tale, a married dad can finally come home—to his waiting wife and daughter.

In Toni Collins's *Willfully Wed*, a sexy private investigator learns who anonymously left a lovely lady a potful of money. But telling the truth could break both their hearts!

Denied his child for years, a single dad wants his son—*and* the woman caring for the boy—in *Substitute Mom* by Maris Soule.

And finally, there's only one thing a bachelor cop with a baby on his hands can do: call for maternal backup in Cara Colter's *Baby in Blue*.

Six wonderful love stories by six talented authors—that's what you'll find this and every month in Silhouette Romance!

Enjoy every one…

Melissa Senate
Senior Editor

Please address questions and book requests to:
Silhouette Reader Service
U.S.: 3010 Walden Ave., P.O. Box 1325, Buffalo, NY 14269
Canadian: P.O. Box 609, Fort Erie, Ont. L2A 5X3

WILLFULLY
WED

Toni Collins

Silhouette

R O M A N C E™

Published by Silhouette Books

America's Publisher of Contemporary Romance

For Sally Schoeneweiss—
as friends go, a class act

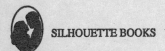

SILHOUETTE BOOKS

ISBN 0-373-19159-6

WILLFULLY WED

Copyright © 1996 by Toni Collins

Printed in U.S.A.

Books by Toni Collins

Silhouette Romance

Ms. Maxwell and Son #664
Letters from Home #893
Something Old #941
Miracle Dad #1008
Miss Scrooge #1050
Willfully Wed #1159

Silhouette Desire

Immoral Support #686

Silhouette Yours Truly

Un*happily* Unwed

TONI COLLINS

is a bestselling author of mainstream novels under her real name. She has worked in numerous occupations, all with one goal in mind: to one day realize her dream of being a full-time writer.

When Ms. Collins began writing for Silhouette Books, she felt a greater freedom with the category romance format, since she felt that she "could do things in these books that simply didn't fit" her mainstream books.

Ms. Collins has traveled extensively and now lives in St. Louis with her son.

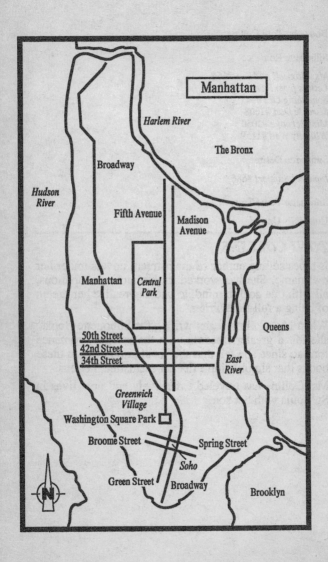

Chapter One

"I had to slap him twice. I thought he was dead."

"That bad?"

"Worse. It's a shame, too—he's one of the best-looking men I've ever met." Danny Vine adjusted the tattered blue baseball cap she wore as she got up to adjust the lighting. "Maybe *the* best, now that I think about it."

As one of the top photographers in New York, Danny Vine was always busy, always in demand. Her professional style was daring, original and colorful—much like the lady herself. Danny—who refused to be called Danielle under any circumstances—was in her late twenties, small and energetic, a woman who stood out in any crowd. Her hair was a long, thick mass of untamed red curls—bright, vibrant red curls, actually. Her eyes were an odd color that was sometimes blue, sometimes green. She dressed to please herself, and the result was more often than not a highly individual look that had nothing to do with fashion or current trends. *Colorful* and *comfortable* best described her personal style.

Danny Vine was one of a kind, and it showed.

It was a trait Phoebe Hatfield had recognized immediately when she first met the brash young photographer seven years ago, and it was the main reason Phoebe had agreed to be Danny's professional representative. Phoebe, unlike Danny, *was* a slave to fashion. Nobody knew better than Phoebe that it was the photographer's special vision that made all the difference in the world. The most expensive equipment available couldn't make up for lack of vision.

Danny had the most unique vision Phoebe had ever encountered. A vision as unique as her look, her personality. Through her eyes, her photographs, one saw even the most familiar things in a whole new light. Her imagination never seemed to have a quiet moment. One of the reasons, Phoebe noted smugly, that Danny was so successful.

Not sure she'd been listening, Danny turned to look at the agent.

"Phoebe?"

Phoebe's head jerked up. "Huh?"

Danny laughed. "You didn't hear a word I said, did you?" she asked, checking the light meter before taking a test shot.

"My mind was on something else," Phoebe admitted reluctantly. Danny was going to make something of that. She always did.

"Something...or someone?" Danny wanted to know, the only aspect of her personality that was predictable.

"Don't start," Phoebe warned, knowing even as she did that it would do no good.

"Don't think I didn't notice the way you were looking at him." Danny checked all of her other cameras to make sure each had been loaded with fresh film.

Phoebe's patience wore thin. "Him? Who?" she asked irritably. What "him" was she being teased about *this* time?

"That guy we met at Planet Hollywood last night." Danny grinned. "As if you don't recall!" Did Phoebe really think she was getting off the hook that easily?

"I don't," her friend insisted.

"Right. And the moon's made of green cheese," Danny sang with a cheerfulness that could be downright disgusting at times. She was almost never in a bad mood. Unfortunately. It tended to make one's own bad moods even harder to tolerate.

"Anyway, we were discussing *your* love life, not mine," Phoebe pointed out. As if either of them actually had one at the moment. Not that Danny didn't get offers. Actually, she got enough for both of them.

"Mine? I don't think so."

"We certainly were," Phoebe insisted. "You were telling me about that gorgeous P.I. you hired."

Danny laughed. "That hardly has anything to do with my love life," she said. "I hired him to check out my so-called inheritance." She wouldn't have minded a more personal relationship, actually.

"You said he was gorgeous," Phoebe prodded.

"Gorgeous, yes, but not my type," Danny assured her. "Too...uh..."

"Stuffy?"

"Something like that, yeah," Danny said, nodding. Something like the understatement of the year. "Fort Knox of the soul." It was the only way she could think of to describe it. In spite of his relaxed look—faded jeans, rolled-up sleeves, slightly long blond hair—he seemed to be anything *but* relaxed. He was a very serious man, no doubt about it. *Intense* was the word that came to mind. Everything seemed to be just beneath the surface with him.

Danny tried not to smile. It wouldn't do to let Phoebe know what she was thinking. It wouldn't do to tell Phoebe that she'd considered asking him to pose for her—partially clad. No, she knew how Phoebe would react. She'd never hear the end of it.

What intrigued her was the possibility of how *he* might react.

"A suit?" Phoebe was asking. Suits, after all, were the worst.

"Not exactly," Danny said, shaking her head. "I mean, he *looks* laid-back enough. He's just hard to read. I couldn't tell where he's really coming from, and it made me nuts." Another understatement. He played his hand so close to the vest even he couldn't see his cards.

Phoebe let out a low whistle. "Looks like he made a definite impression on you," she commented.

"Oh, he made an impression, all right," Danny admitted. He'd made a definite impression on her hormones. It didn't happen often, but when it did, it happened in a major way. Danny did nothing by halves.

"But you hired him anyway."

"Of course I hired him," Danny said. "He's good at what he does." And probably a lot of other things, too, she'd concluded after their first meeting.

"Then he told you he can find out who your benefactor is—was?"

"He practically guaranteed it." Actually, he'd promised only to give it his best shot, but . . .

"I hope this doesn't mean you'll be retiring soon."

Danny adjusted the lights again. "Fat chance," she scoffed. "I could never be idle rich." She could never be idle anything. She was a human whirlwind.

"You never know. With all that money—"

Danny shook her head. "I'm not even sure I'm going to accept it," she said. "It depends pretty much on who it came from—and why." It clearly made a difference.

Phoebe glanced at her watch. "I didn't realize it was so late," she said. "I have to run."

Danny grinned. "Hot date?"

"Hardly. I have a meeting with Gail Edwards at *Vogue*." Phoebe embraced her briefly. "I'll call you."

"Yeah."

After Phoebe was gone, Danny took a letter from her oversize shoulder bag and read it again. How many times had she read it in the past four days? She'd lost track. It didn't make sense. Why would someone leave her an enormous amount of money, but insist that his—or her—identity be kept secret?

This person had to be nuts.

She looked down at the letter and frowned. She couldn't think of anyone who had that kind of money *and* would leave it to her *and* had died recently. One out of three, maybe, but not three out of three, she thought.

Not even two out of three, now that she considered it.

And if it came from someone she *didn't* know . . . Well, that made even less sense. Whoever did it must have had a reason.

What's the catch? she wondered.

She was like no one he'd ever met before.

Words couldn't adequately describe her. *Vibrant,*

exuberant, colorful, ebullient, flamboyant, brash, sassy, sexy—all of those words applied but no one of them alone came close to the true essence of Danny Vine.

Mitchell Newman was alone in his office on Manhattan's Upper West Side. His secretary had gone for the day and the rest of his staff was, for the most part, occupied elsewhere. He was lost in thought, recalling the meeting he'd had that morning with his newest client.

"I'm Danny Vine," she had introduced herself, extending her hand.

He couldn't hide his surprise. "You? But I thought—" he began. He was expecting someone of a completely different, uh...gender.

She finished the sentence for him. "You thought Danny Vine would be a man," she concluded.

"Well, yes," he admitted, embarrassed. To say the least.

She laughed, a full, husky laugh. "Happens all the time," she told him. "I don't like to be called Danielle, so I guess I'll just have to live with it."

He nodded. "What is it that brings you here, Ms. Vine?" he asked.

Whatever it is, I'm eternally grateful, he thought.

"Danny," she corrected. "I dislike formality in any way, shape or form."

He said nothing more, waiting for her to go on. And tried not to stare.

"I got this letter in yesterday's mail," she said, passing it across the desk for his inspection. He took the envelope and opened it.

He read it. It was from a law firm in Chicago. Apparently someone had left her a great deal of money, and for whatever reason, that someone wanted to remain anonymous.

Interesting. Very interesting.

"You want to know who this person was," he concluded.

"Yes," she said, nodding, "and why he or she picked me as an heir."

"*Sole* heir," he corrected, intrigued.

"Even more curious."

"I agree." He paused. This obviously disturbed her. "Do you have reason to be concerned?"

She gave him a puzzled look.

"Do you suspect it might not be entirely legal?" he explained.

Danny Vine drew in a deep breath. "Actually, I never gave that a thought," she admitted. "I just need to know why someone I don't know would leave me so much money and not want me to know who did it."

"Then you're sure it's not someone you know?" he asked.

"I'm not sure of anything," she said, shaking her head. "But why would anyone I know take this route?"

"Why would anyone you *don't* know bequeath you over a million dollars?" he asked.

She seemed to be considering that. Finally she nodded. "Point well taken," she conceded. "I guess there's only one way I'm going to find out, isn't there?"

He explained the cost of his services and what would most likely be involved. She didn't seem to have a problem with any of it. She wrote him a check and asked him to keep her posted.

Now, hours later, he was still thinking about that meeting. She had definitely made an impression on him, but he wasn't quite sure why. She was attractive, sure, but a little too flashy for his tastes.

Not his type. But then, there were times—most of the time, in fact—when he wasn't sure he even had a type. Romance didn't seem to be in the cards for him.

Maybe Joanne had been right, he conceded, thinking of his former fiancée. Maybe he *didn't* know how to love someone.

He'd had no idea there had been a problem until the day Joanne told him she couldn't marry him and returned his ring. What was it she had said? Oh, yeah. He was emotionally remote and didn't know how to love. She didn't believe he loved her.

Joanne wanted passion—affection at the very least. She wanted to hear him say "I love you" at least once a day. Mitch would never understand why women placed so much importance on such silly things. He'd asked her to marry him. He'd bought her a ring, for heaven's sake! Wasn't that proof enough?

He'd concluded that Joanne, as beautiful and successful as she was, was basically insecure—too much so for him. It was her problem, not his.

Now he wasn't so sure.

Danny Vine was the reason he was starting to doubt himself. She'd stirred something in him he didn't know existed until she walked into his office that morning. This was a woman who'd stand out anywhere, with all that red hair, so vividly red, and that free, uninhibited manner. Even the way she was dressed was a reflection of her unique personality: purple suede boots and leggings, with a big hot-pink sweater that drooped off one shoulder and was belted with what he was convinced were two dog collars buckled together. The only jewelry she wore was an unusually large wristwatch that appeared to be about as big as Big Ben and dangling earrings comprised of bits of multicolored glass. She wore a black baseball cap and a purple wool cape.

Not his type. Still . . .

Everything about her intrigued him, but he dismissed that as no more than a simple reaction to a woman who was so dramatically different from the women he was accustomed to. He reached for the jar of peppermints on the desk, unwrapped one, and popped it into his mouth thoughtfully.

He looked down at her client file lying on the desk in front of him. The label read D. VINE. Mitch smiled to himself.

It was the understatement of the year.

"Danny, phone!"

Danny waved off the assistant brandishing the cordless telephone. He knew better than to interrupt her during a shoot. "Take a message, Dennis," she called back to him.

"I tried. He says it's urgent, has to talk to you now."

She let out an exaggerated groan. "Did you at least get his name?" she wanted to know.

"Mitch somebody."

She stopped what she was doing. "Mitchell Newman?" she asked.

"Yeah, that's it."

Danny straightened up and handed her camera to another assistant, then turned to the two male models. "At ease," she said with a dismissive wave of her hand, then crossed the studio to take the phone from Dennis.

"This is Danny. Talk to me," she said briskly.

There was a pause on the other end of the line. "Ms. Vine, this is Mitchell Newman," he said finally.

She snorted disdainfully. "I thought I told you I don't like to be called Ms. Vine."

"So you did."

"What's up?"

"I contacted the law firm in Chicago," he told her.

"And?"

"A waste of time."

"They wouldn't tell you anything?"

"Nothing. Not that it comes as any kind of surprise," he said. "If they hadn't been instructed to protect their client's identity, they would have told you up front who left you the money. They have their orders."

"So where do we go from here?" Danny asked.

"That's what I'd like to discuss with you," he said gravely.

"Shoot."

"Not over the phone," he said. "Can you come by my office this afternoon?"

She hesitated. Bad news? Why couldn't he tell her over the phone? It smelled an awful lot like bad news to her. "What time?" she asked finally.

"Two o'clock all right for you?"

"I'll be there."

She broke the connection and stared at the phone for a long moment. Something didn't feel right about this, hadn't felt right from the beginning. It just didn't make sense.

Maybe I should just tell them I'm not accepting the money and get it over with, she thought. It's not worth the trouble.

"Danny?"

The sound of Phoebe's voice interrupted her thoughts. "Phoebe," she said, forcing a smile she didn't much feel. "What're you doing here?"

"I come bearing good news," Phoebe answered her.

"Great. I could use some."

"What's wrong?"

"The gumshoe just called," Danny said, making a face.

Phoebe frowned. "Problems?"

"You could say that." Danny sighed heavily. "This whole business is so fishy you could wrap it in newspaper and serve it with chips."

Phoebe stifled a chuckle. Danny's way with words had always amused her. "Well," she began as she put down her alligator bag—an accessory Danny had long considered appropriate for someone of her capabilities. "I think what I have for you will take your mind off your troubles, at least for a little while."

"And what might that be?" Danny asked dubiously.

"You got the centerfold job." Phoebe was beaming like a proud mother, but Danny figured it probably wouldn't do to tell her that. "You're going to be photographing three of the hottest hunks around."

"Wonderful."

"I thought you'd be thrilled."

"I am thrilled," Danny insisted. "I've just got a lot on my mind, that's all."

The cartwheels, she decided, would have to wait.

* * *

"What is it you couldn't discuss with me over the phone?" Danny asked, removing her cape.

She'd outdone herself this time, Mitch decided. Lime green tights with a long turquoise tunic. Around her neck were a multitude of silver chains of varying weights and lengths. The leather band on her watch was pink. Against his will, he was turned on. And he was sure it was exactly the response she always aimed for.

This was a woman who liked attention. No doubt about it. Everything about her out there for the world to see.

"Sit down," he told her.

She did. "Now tell me."

"First of all," he began, "I need to ask you a few questions."

"Like what?"

"Like can you think of anyone who might have reason to leave you that kind of money?" he asked.

She frowned. "If I could, I wouldn't have needed to hire you, now, would I?" she asked irritably, fingering her hair.

He didn't respond right away. "I had to ask," he said tightly.

"Well, I can't!" she snapped. "Nobody I'm close to died recently. I haven't been to any funerals in the past few months."

"Perhaps someone from your childhood, someone you haven't seen in years?"

Danny shook her head. "Not likely," she insisted.

"But possible?"

"Anything is possible," Danny conceded. "But I wouldn't bet on it."

"A distant relative?" He had to consider all the possibilities.

"Nope."

"Maybe a friend of the family?" he asked. "Someone without children of their own?"

Danny leaned back in the chair, propping her feet up on one corner of his desk. "That wouldn't make sense," she said.

"Why not?"

"I come from a large family—nine children," she explained. "Why would anyone who was a friend of the family leave me over a million dollars, but nothing to my brothers and sisters?"

She was wearing ballet slippers. Black ones. And he was staring at her legs, unable to stop. He felt like an idiot. "I see," he finally managed.

"This is hopeless, isn't it?" she asked.

"I didn't say that."

"I know you didn't. I did."

"It's not hopeless," he assured her, "but it's not going to be easy."

"Obviously."

"It's going to take time."

"How much time?"

He shook his head. "Hard to say," he answered honestly.

"Do I have to accept the bequest within a set time limit?" she asked.

"I would assume so," he said. "I can check it out, if you like."

"Yes." She straightened up, removing her legs from his view. "Please do."

"Whether you accept it depends on why it was left to you, then?" he asked.

"Of course it does," she told him. "Would you accept that kind of money if you didn't know who left it to you—or why?"

"I'm not sure I'd accept it even if I did know," he answered honestly.

"Neither am I." She stood up. "I have this thing about unanswered questions."

"Obviously."

"I like to know who I'm indebted to."

"I don't believe there are any strings attached to this bequest," he said.

"Sure there are," Danny disagreed. "I'm not supposed to know who left it to me, or why." She reached for her cape, wrapping it around her shoulders in one quick, sweeping motion.

He was staring again—and furious with himself for doing so. She was incredible. Absolutely incredible. And no doubt trouble.

"Is something wrong?" she asked.

It took him a moment to realize that she'd noticed the way he was looking at her. It took a moment longer for him to realize that she was smiling.

That she obviously liked it.

Mentally, he reminded himself—for the hundredth time—that she was a client. *A client.*

Therefore, she was off limits. Still . . .

"So where do we go from here?" she asked.

"Huh?"

"I said, where do we go from here?" she asked again.

It took him a few seconds to pull his thoughts together. "Well, uh, first I think I'd better find out how much time you have to make up your mind."

She nodded slowly, apparently waiting for him to continue.

He felt like an idiot. A world-class idiot.

"And?"

"I'll have to give that some thought. This person—whoever he or she is—has covered their tracks extremely well."

She sighed heavily. "Yes."

"Beyond that . . ." He shrugged.

Fool! he mentally berated himself.

"I don't get it," she said as she headed for the door. "Why couldn't you discuss this with me over the phone?"

"Confidentiality" was the only excuse he could come up with on short notice. He wasn't about to tell her that he was so intrigued, he just wanted to see her again.

He thought about it after she had gone. He could have discussed it with her over the phone. He hadn't because he didn't want to.

He wanted her to come here, to his office.

He wanted to see her again.

Fool, he mentally reprimanded himself. Getting involved with a client was the absolute worst thing a P.I. could do.

And getting involved with the likes of Danny Vine would be insanity.

Especially for him.

Chapter Two

At the Vine family home in Troy, New York, a typical family get-together was in full swing. As usual, attendance was one hundred percent, which made for a crowded, very noisy house.

It was the one thing Danny had missed most when she moved away to New York City. The one thing she still missed. So what if she'd had to wait in line for the bathroom and make sure she wasn't late for dinner in order to get her share? It might have been frustrating at the time, but she'd still been happy, and she was certain her siblings had been happy, too.

All eight of them.

Danny was the youngest. The eldest, Camille, was an interior designer, married to one of her clients, a real estate developer. The triplets, Michael, Eugene and Nicholas, were all still single. Michael was an attorney, Eugene a pilot and Nicholas worked for the telephone company. Karyn was a teacher, married but with no children and showing no signs of wanting any. Meryl was an independent filmmaker, happily married; her pets were her kids—three dogs, all spoiled rotten. Christiane was a struggling actress who, at the moment, was doing commercials. Sally was a copywriter for an advertising agency in Boston.

A big, happy, noisy family.

They raised us right, Danny thought, watching her parents across the room. We were brought up with just the right amount of love and discipline.

"It isn't like you to be so quiet, Danny." This was Sally. A petite blonde, she looked nothing like Danny. But then, none of them really did.

Danny turned to her sister. "I was just thinking," she said. "Do you remember any of us ever getting a spanking when we were kids?"

Sally thought about it. "No, I can't say that I do," she said finally.

"Do you think we were just that good, or were they just that lenient?" Danny wondered aloud.

Sally laughed. "They just didn't believe in corporal punishment," she answered with certainty. "No parent is ever lucky enough to have all good kids, especially in a family as large as ours."

"And especially with three boys like Mike, Gene and Nick," Danny agreed, nodding. They, she recalled, had needed it.

"Did I just hear someone taking my name in vain?" Nick asked, grinning broadly as he joined them.

"We never take your name any other way," Danny assured him.

"I'm wounded," he said, feigning hurt as he gripped his chest to make a point.

"What are you three up to now?" their father asked, clearly amused.

"The usual," Danny told him. It never ceased to strike her how amazing her parents were—in every way. Well into their fifties now, they were both still quite attractive. They took care of themselves—they were active and ate right, habits all nine of their children had learned by example.

"Nicholas, what are you doing to your sisters now?" their mother wanted to know. She knew her son only too well.

He rolled his eyes upward. "Why do you always think it's me, Mom?" he asked.

Danny grinned, knowing he didn't really need to ask.

She smiled. "Because it always is, dear," she told him.

"Now, that's not true—"

"I'm afraid it is," Millie Vine disagreed, "and has been since all of you were children."

Sally turned to Danny. "See what I mean?"

Danny grinned. "Some things never change, do they?" This much hadn't changed, anyway, not since they were kids.

After a few minutes, both Sally and Nick moved on to catch up with other family members, leaving Danny alone with her parents. When she'd answered all the usual questions asked at these get-togethers, she decided to ask a question of her own.

"Do either of you know anyone who'd leave me a lot of money?" she questioned them.

She thought they'd laugh, but they didn't. They looked at Danny, then at each other, with unmasked surprise. "Where's this coming from, Danny?" her father asked. Her mother remained silent, frowning.

"This." She took the letter from her bag and handed it to him.

He read it, with his wife reading over his shoulder. Danny was puzzled by the odd expressions on their faces when they looked up at her. "No," her father said, handing it back to her. "I can't think of anyone."

Her mother shook her head emphatically. "No, neither can I."

They were saying no, but doing so in such an obviously uneasy manner that it made Danny uncomfortable, too. Why were they uneasy? she asked herself. *Why* would this bother them—and she could tell it did—if they didn't know of anyone who might leave her a large sum of money?

"This is weird," she said aloud, raking a hand through her thick red hair—a gesture of frustration. "Somebody's trying to give me a lot of money. There has to be a reason why."

Her parents looked nervous. But why?

"I'm sure there is, dear, but I don't know anyone who would have done so," her mother maintained.

"Perhaps this is someone you've dealt with professionally," her father suggested.

Danny shook her head. "I have friends on the professional level, sure, but no one who'd have that kind of money to leave to me or anyone else. Besides, no one I've worked with has passed away recently."

Her parents both frowned. "I'm sure you'll find out who your benefactor is, dear," Millie told her.

"So am I," Danny answered confidently. "I've hired a private investigator."

Harris and Millie exchanged curiously worried looks.

"It seems like the only way to find out," Danny went on to explain. Their behavior was making her nervous.

"Does it really matter?" her father asked.

"Of course it matters!" Danny responded, surprised by the question. "Someone wants to give me all this money. You'd better believe I want to know who."

"You know what they say about not looking a gift horse in the mouth," Nick said as he walked past them.

"A cliché," Danny shot back at him. "And don't forget about the Trojan horse."

"Why is knowing who left the money important to you?" her father questioned.

This wasn't like her father at all, and it bothered Danny more than she let on. Harris Vine was a brilliant attorney, a brilliant judge, because he'd always questioned everything. Unanswered questions were simply not allowed, not in his courtroom.

What gives? Danny wondered.

"I don't have anything else to report—yet," Mitch told Danny as he admitted her to his private office a few days later.

"I might." She removed her cape, revealing electric blue leggings and a hot-pink tunic. And lots of silver jewelry.

He gave her a quizzical look as she walked past him and seated herself.

The lady was full of surprises.

"Meaning exactly what?" he asked carefully as he walked around his desk and sat down.

"Something weird happened over the weekend."

"Weird?" That was the same way he could describe the reaction he always had to her. Mentally he reprimanded himself.

"Very weird."

"In what way?" He knew he was staring at her but was unable to stop.

"I spent the weekend at home—that is, at my parents' home in upstate New York," she explained. "I showed them the letter."

"You hadn't mentioned it to them before?" This surprised him.

Why? he wondered.

She shook her head. "No," she said. "Frankly, I was surprised by the way they reacted. They were nervous—*very* nervous."

"Any idea why?"

"Not a clue," she admitted. "When I told them I hired you, they really freaked."

"Freaked?" he asked. That was not the kind of response to be dismissed without scrutiny.

"They were upset. Oh, they tried not to let it show, but I could tell," she recalled. "They advised me not to worry about it, about where it came from or why."

"This is an unusual response?" Mitch questioned her.

She nodded. "For them it is," she answered. "My father's a circuit court judge. He's never taken anything at face value, not as far as I can remember."

"And your mother?"

"She's more trusting than Dad—that is, she's more likely to accept things at face value, but she's no pushover, either," Danny said. "They were both much too quick to accept this whole business without question. Or rather, they were too quick to urge *me* to accept it."

"You think they know something, then," he concluded.

"I'm not sure," she admitted. "It just doesn't feel right."

"You want me to investigate your parents?" he asked then.

"No!" She looked shocked that he would even suggest such a thing. It was, he realized, the first time he'd gotten such a reaction from her.

"Calm down," he told her. "I wasn't talking about digging up dirt on them."

"You wouldn't find any," she assured him.

"If you say so." Given their response to her inheritance, he wasn't so sure. "I was only suggesting looking into their backgrounds, the people they've known and associated with, to see if we can find someone who might have been behind your inheritance."

"That wouldn't make sense."

"Why not?" he asked, curious.

"We've been through this before," she pointed out. "I have eight brothers and sisters. If anyone were close enough to my parents to make such a gesture, they would have left it to all of us, not just me."

"Not if their connections was *only* to you," he disagreed.

"How so?" she asked, puzzled.

"Do you have godparents?"

She nodded. "But they're both still living."

"A favorite aunt or uncle?" he suggested.

She thought about it. "Two aunts and an uncle, but they're still alive."

"Grandparents?"

"This is silly," she stated, frustrated. "They're gone, but why would they leave their money only to me? Why would they try to keep it a secret?"

"Stranger things have happened." He spoke from experience, though she didn't know it.

"Maybe I should just refuse the bequest and avoid all the hassles and headaches," she said after giving it some thought.

"You don't want that."

She looked at him. "How do you know what I want or don't want?" she asked.

"If you didn't want the money, if you didn't want to know who left it to you, you wouldn't have come this far," he reminded her.

"I want to know who left it to me," she admitted. "I don't like unanswered questions. But I'm beginning to wonder if knowing is worth the hassle."

"And the money?"

"Money doesn't mean all that much to me," she told him. "I don't care about being rich. I care about being comfortable."

He studied her for a moment. She meant it. She really meant it. A woman who truly did not care about money. She was even more unique than he thought.

"So, you meant it when you told me you weren't sure you'd accept the bequest, even if you did find out who it was from."

She nodded.

He drew in a deep breath. "I'll keep digging," he told her.

She smiled. "You do that."

In spite of his own ironclad rule about not mixing business with pleasure, not getting emotionally involved with his clients, he wanted to ask her out. Danny Vine was special. Unique. He'd be a fool to let her get away.

So he was a fool.

Instead of asking her out, he escorted her through the outer office to the door, promising to be in touch. After she was gone, he turned to his secretary.

"I'm an idiot," he told her.

Shirley looked up from the bill she was typing. "It sure took you long enough to figure that one out," she said in her high-pitched, nasal voice.

He made a face. "Thanks for the vote of confidence," he said, pretending to be more annoyed than he actually was.

"Come on, Mitch," she told him. "You've got it bad for her. It stands out like the neon lights in Times Square. But you don't do anything about it. That's dumb, no matter how you slice it."

Shirley didn't look like a philosopher by any stretch of the imagination—she was a rather voluptuous brunette who always dressed to show off her curves—but she'd been known to make some astute observations on life and love.

Especially love.

"So what is it *you* think I should do, Shirl?" he asked.

"Try doing what comes naturally," she suggested.

His eyes widened. "I beg your pardon?"

"Ask her out, Studley Do-Right," she advised.

"You know my policy when it comes to mixing business with pleasure," he reminded her.

"Yeah, and I know the way you look at *her,* too," Shirley said with a knowing smile. "You know what they say about rules being made to be broken."

He made a face. "You're not making this easy for me," he said.

"You're not making this easy for yourself," she disagreed. "Loosen up. Live a little."

He shook his head. "Is that what you do?" he asked. "Live a little?"

"Me? Nah," she said with a dismissive wave of her hand. "I live a *lot!*"

"I'll just bet you do," he said with a chuckle as he headed back into his office. Sometimes he wished Shirley were a little less outspoken.

The truth hurt.

"He'd make a fabulous centerfold model," Danny stated with the certainty of a gourmet tasting a flawless dish. She'd certainly like to put that theory to the test.

Her closest friend, Anna Chadwick, sat on the floor cross-legged, looking as though she might start chanting at any moment. "When did that become one of the criteria for hiring a P.I.?" she questioned.

Anna and Danny had been friends since they were children. The Vines and the Chadwicks had been next-door neighbors in Troy for as long as either Danny or Anna could remember. Now they were neighbors in New York—in the same apartment building. Anna, a set designer for a long-running Broadway show, was even more flamboyant than Danny. With her long, thick blond curls reaching well past her shoulders, her large, one-of-a-kind jewelry and her vivid, dramatic clothes, she made Danny seem almost conservative.

"Danny?"

She jerked. "Huh?"

"I asked if that was a new requirement for a good P.I."

"It's not a requirement, Anna, it's a bonus," Danny told her. "A very definite bonus."

"So far it doesn't seem to have been much of a bonus for you," Anna observed, reaching for the herbal tea Danny poured for her. "He hasn't asked you out yet, has he?"

Danny shook her head. "No, he hasn't," she admitted. "But that's a situation I'm about to rectify."

Anna raised an eyebrow. "How so?" she asked.

"I'm going to ask him out," Danny said promptly. "I thought I'd invite him to dinner—someplace where he can have steak. I'm sure he's the steak-and-potatoes type. I thought about getting tickets for a show, but I doubt that's something he'd enjoy."

"You seem awfully sure of yourself," Anna observed, sipping her tea. "You sure he's going to accept your invitation?"

Danny nodded. "Pretty sure, yes," she answered without hesitation. "I can tell by the way he acts, by the way he reacts to me."

"That obvious?"

"That obvious," Danny maintained. "He wants to, I know he does."

"No brag, just fact, huh?" Anna asked, amused.

"I'm not being vain," Danny defended herself. "There are things—well, you know. A woman can just tell sometimes." And, she thought, there are things that just can't be put into words without tripping over your tongue.

"I suppose," Anna said with a halfhearted nod.

"Haven't you ever been in this situation before?" Danny asked, reaching for one of the fudge truffle cookies on the platter with the teapot.

"Maybe. Once or twice," Anna conceded.

"Then you know what I mean." Danny bit into the cookie.

Anna gave her blond curls a toss. "I suppose. But then I'm not as in tune to the male psyche as you are," she said wryly.

"Very funny."

"It's true, isn't it?"

Danny shrugged. "I don't know. I never really thought about it." It was the truth; she'd never thought of herself as a femme fatale by any means. She did think that when men described her as sexy they were merely sensing what she felt inside. She *felt* sexy—that was an attitude, not a look.

Now that she'd thought about it, she *still* didn't consider herself a femme fatale.

"Earth to Danny. Earth to Danny."

The sound of Anna's voice cut through her thoughts. "Huh?"

"I asked you how you found this guy," Anna said, apparently for the second time.

"In the yellow pages."

"The yellow pages!" Anna burst into laughter.

"I needed a P.I. He had the biggest ad," Danny said. "He stood out."

"Obviously."

The phone rang then. "Just a minute," she said as she reached for it. "This is Danny. Talk to me."

"Danny, this is Mitch Newman," said the husky male voice on the other end of the line.

"Hi, what's up?" Turning to face Anna, she mouthed the words, "It's him."

"A couple of questions—about your parents."

"Uh-huh?"

"Were either of them ever married before?"

"Married before they were married to each other, you mean?" She wondered where this was leading.

"Yeah."

"No."

"You're sure about that?"

"Of course I am!" she was more than a little annoyed with this, and with him. "What's the point, Newman?"

"Is it possible that either of your parents might not be your biological parent?" he asked bluntly.

Danny was appalled. "No, it is not!" she snapped.

"Look, I'm not trying to upset you—"

She cut him off, responding angrily. "I'd hate to see what would happen if you *were* trying, then!"

"I'm going to have to ask questions like this if I'm ever going to find out who left you the money," he told her.

"Well, you're looking in the wrong direction!"

"Then neither of your parents has ever been married before."

"No."

"Neither of them has ever been intimately involved with anyone else?"

"Certainly not!"

"You're sure about that?"

"Absolutely!"

"How do you know?"

"I know my parents," she said firmly. "They are and always have been totally devoted to each other. There's never been anyone else for either of them." She paused. "Why are you even asking me this?"

"I told you." His voice stayed calm. "You said they both reacted oddly when you told them about this."

"Yes, they did," she acknowledged.

"You also pointed out that if the bequest had come from a relative, it would have been left to all the children," he went on.

"That's right."

"But it would make sense if this person were only related to you," he said then.

"Not possible," she insisted. "Even if either of my parents had been married before, I'm the youngest of their children—not the oldest."

"There has to be something we're both overlooking," he said, perplexed.

"Brilliant deduction, Sherlock," she said with a tinge of sarcasm in her voice.

As she hung up, she found herself wondering if she'd made a mistake. Then she thought of his eyes, his smile, his great body.

I hope not, she thought.

Chapter Three

"It's been a while, Mitchell."

"Not by choice," Mitch assured his grandfather. "Just been busy, that's all."

"I don't doubt it." Joseph Markham, a retired New York circuit judge, never bothered to conceal his special feelings for his grandson. That, Mitch decided, was probably why he'd always gravitated toward him, even as a small child. His grandfather gave him what his own father had always denied him: affection.

And love.

Normally, Mitch joined his grandfather for dinner at his brownstone on the upper East Side at least once a week, but lately Mitch's schedule had been so hectic, he'd had to cancel more often than he showed up. He regretted it. His grandfather was the only family he had now—at least he was the only family that really felt like family.

My father certainly doesn't feel like family, he thought now.

"Maybe things would have been different if Elizabeth had lived," Joseph suggested, as if reading his mind.

Elizabeth Markham Newman, Joseph's daughter and Mitch's mother, had died when Mitch was only two years old, the victim of a drunk driver. His memories of her were vague at best. The only mother he'd had growing up was the full-length painting in the entry hall at that museum masquerading as a home—a painting of a beautiful, elegant woman whose eyes reflected a deep sadness. Mitch had gotten to know his mother through his grandfather. His father never talked about her at all.

His father never had the time.

Mitch frowned thoughtfully. "I doubt anything would change Randall Newman," he said finally, calling his father by name because somehow "Father" just didn't suit the man who'd sired him.

And "Dad" certainly didn't. Not by any stretch of the imagination.

"Your mother loved you, Mitchell," his grandfather said as his longtime housekeeper, Gladys, started to serve their dinner.

Gladys, a plump, pleasant woman in her mid-sixties, had been with Joseph Markham over twenty-five years and was totally devoted to him. She'd learned all of Mitch's favorite dishes and made a point of preparing them whenever he came for dinner. Tonight she'd made cheese lasagna with garlic bread and salad with creamy Italian dressing. "And your favorite dessert," she promised.

"Elizabeth loved you more than anything in the world," Joseph said.

Mitch was genuinely surprised by his grandfather's statement. "I don't doubt that, Granddad, not for a minute," he assured the older man. "All I meant was that nothing could change the old man."

The older man shook his head sadly. "I never understood what she saw in him," Joseph admitted with a heavy sigh. "I tried to talk her out of marrying him, but she was so sure she'd found the man of her dreams." He shook his head sadly. "Turned out to be more of a nightmare than a dream."

"No better at being a husband than he was at being a father, is that it?" Mitch asked. He had no way of knowing what kind of husband Randall Newman had been, but it came as no surprise to him that he hadn't been any better at that than he'd been as a father.

Joseph frowned. "He was never there for her when she needed him," he recalled. "I think she saw more of him before they were married, actually."

More common ground we share, Mitch decided. Neither of us is a fan of my father.

Joseph, he knew only too well, blamed Randall for Elizabeth's death. He was convinced she would not have been out on the street that night had they not argued, had she not been so upset.

Had she not finally had enough.

"She must have loved him," Mitch concluded. Only love could have prompted her to stay with him. Mitch knew this because it was the only thing that had kept him from running away as a child. He'd loved his father—or tried to, anyway. Only when he was old enough to realize the love he gave his father was being wasted did he finally give up.

Joseph nodded. "That she did, though I'll never know why," he said, taking a bite. "Randall was all business—in more ways than one. He never thought of anyone or anything but himself and his law practice. He was always too busy to even take her out to dinner unless it was a business dinner. If she wanted to spend time with him, she had to invite one of his partners or clients along."

"That didn't work for me," Mitch recalled, thinking of all the lonely nights he'd spent alone in his room while his father was out at one of his all too frequent business dinners. Long, lonely nights spent wishing his father would notice him at all.

"You couldn't play hostess," Joseph pointed out.

"I couldn't do much of anything as far as Randall was concerned," Mitch told his grandfather. "Nothing I did pleased him."

"He had no idea what to do with you." Joseph paused as Gladys served dessert, a hot peach cobbler topped with French vanilla ice cream. "A child didn't fit into his plans. Elizabeth was at least a professional asset—she was beautiful, if I do say so myself. She was intelligent. She had poise. She could accompany him to social functions with the clients and the partners and all. She could arrange dinner parties. But what could he do with a child?"

Mitch's jaw tightened. The answer, unfortunately, was obvious. "Just what he did. Nothing," he said darkly. "I don't know why he even kept me."

"I wish I could say he really did care but just didn't quite know how to deal with having to raise a child, but frankly, I was never sure about anything where Randall was concerned," Joseph admitted. "I think since you were a boy, he did see you as a future law partner. A girl would most likely have been groomed to fill Elizabeth's role as hostess."

Mitch concentrated on his cobbler for a few thoughtful moments. "In other words, I would eventually have been of value to him, had I stuck around."

"If you'd gone to law school, as he wanted, yes."

Mitch shook his head. "Not exactly unconditional love, was it?" he asked.

"Randall never gave anyone anything unconditionally," Joseph responded honestly.

Mitch had always appreciated his grandfather's honesty—even when it hurt. At least he'd always known where he stood with Joseph. With his father, he'd always been uncertain.

There was a long, thoughtful silence.

"I met someone," he said aloud, breaking the stillness.

Joseph was surprised, and seemed to be pleased, as well. "A woman? It's about time," he said, smiling broadly.

Mitch laughed. "Did I say it was a woman?" he asked.

The older man's smile vanished. "Don't tell me you were referring to a man!" He looked alarmed.

Mitch laughed even harder. "No, I definitely was *not* referring to a man," he reassured his grandfather. "I was referring to a client."

Joseph was clearly concerned. "That's not a good idea," he warned.

Mitch frowned. As if he had to be told. "Tell me about it," he said. "I know all about the potential risks and pitfalls. But this is the first time in a long time I've met anyone who..." He trailed off, feeling oddly foolish making such a confession, even to his grandfather.

"Who is she?" Joseph asked.

"Her name is Danny—Danielle, actually—and she's a photographer," Mitch told him. "She recently inherited a very large sum of money from someone who doesn't want his or her identity known."

"Curious," Joseph acknowledged with a nod, waiting for him to say more.

"More than a little," Mitch agreed.

"Any leads?"

Mitch shook his head. "They've all been dead ends—so far."

"Tell me about her, Mitchell," his grandfather said then. "What is it about her that you find so fascinating?"

"Everything." Mitch summed it up without hesitation. "She's a very unique woman, Granddad— attractive, spirited, independent. No slave to fashion, that's for sure, but she'd stand out in any crowd. She doesn't really care about the money. She won't take the inheritance without knowing who left it to her and why. Maybe not even then."

His grandfather smiled. "That is unique," he agreed. "Have you been seeing her—socially, I mean?"

Mitch shook his head. "I've been wrestling with the matter of ethics," he said. "There's no written law that says I can't ask her out—it's not like I'm a doctor or anything like that—and I really would like to."

"But?"

"As you know, I don't have the best track record with women," he pointed out.

"You haven't really worked at it, Mitchell," Joseph reminded him. 'You haven't put forth the effort. Apparently you consider this woman worth the effort.''

"I've always harbored a secret fear that genetics might be working against me," Mitch confided, not yet willing to admit, even to his grandfather just what he considered Danny to be worth.

"By genetics, you mean your father?"

He made a wry face. "Who else?"

"Being your father's son doesn't necessarily mean you're your father's son, Mitchell."

Mitch gave him a quizzical look.

"Just because you're Randall Newman's son doesn't mean you're going to be like him," Joseph clarified. "Having had the kind of childhood you had, you could turn out to be a model husband and father. You could be like your mother, you know."

"Having the kind of profession I have, I seriously doubt it."

His grandfather gave him a suspicious look. "It sounds to me like you're making excuses," he observed.

"Right." His grandfather knew him too well.

"Aren't you?"

"No. Of course not." It wouldn't do any good to deny it.

"Then why are you being so defensive?" Joseph challenged.

"I'm not."

"That's not the way it sounds."

Or looks, I'll wager, Mitch thought miserably.

"I'm frustrated. Don't read too much into it," he told him.

"You're nothing like your father, Mitchell," his grandfather reassured him. "You got more than your looks from your mother."

Mitch frowned. He wished he could remember his mother.

If only she'd lived . . .

She was getting to him.

Danny Vine was driving Mitch totally nuts without even trying, without even knowing she was doing it. Or did she?

Could she know?

Could she have a clue?

He drew in a deep breath. Did she suspect, even for a moment, the effect she had on him?

He hoped not. He hoped he was better at covering himself than that.

I wouldn't be much of a P.I. if I'm not, he thought.

Mixing business and pleasure was a bad idea. A real bad idea, he told himself. If he hadn't believed that before, he believed it now. He hadn't been able to get her out of his mind since he met her. And he hadn't been very effective in dealing with her case since his libido kept getting in the way. Not good. Not good at all.

That was almost as frustrating as wanting Danny and not being able to do anything about it.

Almost, but not quite.

Maybe he'd be better off if he just resigned from the case and asked her out.

That was, after all, what he really wanted to do, if he were to be totally honest with himself. That and much more.

Stupid idea, he thought dismally. He was the long shot in the relationship derby. If he resigned from the case, she might—*might*—go out with him once, and that would be it.

Or would it?

Did they have any kind of a chance at having a real relationship?

He doubted it.

Expect the worst and you never get disappointed, he told himself.

"Jeez, what planet are you on?"

He jerked around. His secretary had come into his office and was standing on the other side of the desk, eyeing him suspiciously. Sometimes he was convinced she was psychic.

"What?" he asked, distracted.

"I asked, what planet are you on?" she repeated.

He turned to look at her. There were times when Shirley could be a sight for sore eyes. Most of the time, though, she was a sight that caused sore eyes. She went out of her way to achieve a costume effect and succeeded in a major way.

"I don't know. What planet *am* I on?" he wanted to know.

"One that doesn't require gray matter, obviously."

"Funny. Did you intrude for any particular reason?" he asked.

"Yeah," she responded with a nod. "I got these ready for your signature." She held up a stack of letters.

"I'll get to them a little later," he said, turning back to the window.

"You'll get to them now," she said firmly. "I've got to take this stuff to the post office on my lunch hour."

Pushy, as always.

"Can't it wait?"

She shook her head emphatically. "Nope."

"Not even a few minutes?" She shook her head again.

I'm not going to win this one, he decided. Reluctantly, he turned back to the desk again, scribbling his signature on each of the letters, acutely aware that Shirley was staring at him.

"Is there a problem, Shirl?"

"Want to talk about it?" she asked finally.

"About what?" he asked, deciding it would be smart to play dumb. Lie very still, he thought, and maybe she'll just sniff you and go away.

"You know what I'm talking about," she insisted.

"Shirley—"

"It's her, isn't it?"

"Her?"

"The redhead." Shirley perched on one corner of his desk. "You've really got it bad for her, don't you?"

Play dumb, Newman.

"I have no idea what you're talking about, Shirley," he responded evasively.

Maybe she'll take the hint, he thought hopefully.

No such luck.

"Like heck you don't!" Shirley laughed. "C'mon, Boss, fess up."

"Shirley, this is personal," he began. He really didn't want to get into this with her, but he doubted she was going to give him much of a choice.

"You think I don't know that?"

He raised an eyebrow. "Apparently not," he concluded.

Take the hint, Shirl.

"I'm right, aren't I?" she asked, not about to give up.

Unfortunately, Shirley *never* gave up. She had the tenacity of a hungry bulldog.

Mitch studied her for a moment. "What makes you so sure I've 'got it bad,' as you put it, for Danny Vine?" he asked, wondering just how obvious he really was.

If Shirley had noticed, Danny might also have noticed.

"If you wore a neon sign it couldn't be any more obvious," she said, almost as if she'd read his mind.

"Thanks," he groaned. "Just what I needed to hear."

Just what I don't need to hear.

She shrugged. "You asked."

"Maybe I shouldn't have."

Definitely I shouldn't have.

"Tell me something, Boss," Shirley started carefully.

"What?"

Here it comes. Ready or not.

"You obviously *want* to, so why don't you do anything about it?" she asked.

He shook his head. "I wish I knew," he confessed.

"Ask her out," Shirley urged.

He managed a slight smile. "Just like that?" he asked.

Shirley nodded. "Just like that."

"Right."

Hopping off the desk, Shirley headed for the door. Mitch didn't notice. He was deep in thought, where he remained for several minutes.

"That's it, Kim, look into Michael's eyes!" Danny called out to the two models. "Let's see some passion! Don't worry about the hair! This is a shampoo ad. We *want* to see lots of hair blowing in the wind!"

They were on the eighty-sixth-floor observation deck on the Empire State Building, where Danny was shooting an advertisement for a new shampoo that was to appear in all the major women's magazines. The models were clad in the latest fashions, but Danny wore faded jeans, a tattered baseball jacket and cap and a pair of well-traveled tennis shoes. Only Danny would have the self-confidence to do that. But then, she was among friends. She'd worked with both of the models before and knew them to be totally professional, but today they seemed distracted. Or maybe she was the one who was distracted. Her mind certainly wasn't one hundred percent on the shoot, as it should have been, as it normally was.

It was on Mitch Newman.

"Hey, Danny!" one of her assistants called out to her. "There's somebody here to see you!"

Great, she thought. Whoever it is, his timing stinks. Frustrated, Danny signaled to the models to take a break. Just what I *don't* need, she thought as she put the camera down and turned to greet the visitor with a smile she didn't really feel like.

That forced smile vanished when she saw it was Mitch Newman. Lately, every time they spoke to each other they ended up arguing. Why, she found herself wondering again, was he so sure her parents had something to do with all of this?

He'd probably ask why she was so sure they didn't. At any rate, she was sure she was about to find out.

"Danny."

He was smiling. A good sign? she wondered. "Hi, Mitch. What's up?" She tried to sound nonchalant even though she was feeling anything but. She hoped he didn't notice.

"Nothing. Yet," he responded. He didn't look out of place here, but he sure acted like he felt that way.

"Nothing? Then what brings you here?" she asked.

"You," he answered, getting right to the point. "I wanted to see if you're free for dinner."

"Tonight?" She was surprised and didn't bother to hide it.

Dinner? He's up to something.

"Hopefully."

She raised an eyebrow. "A business dinner?" she asked, hoping he'd say no.

Mitch shook his head. "Strictly personal," he assured her.

She truly smiled for the first time that day. "In that case, I accept," she told him.

"You sound relieved that it's not business," he noted.

"I am. This whole business is making me nuts," she admitted. "I'm this close to just saying forget the whole thing and refusing the inheritance." Holding up one hand, she indicated a very short distance between her thumb and forefinger.

"You don't mean that."

"I've never meant anything more in my life," she assured him.

"Don't you want to know who left you all that money—and why?" he asked, more than a little curious himself.

"Sure. But not at the expense of my sanity." She took off her baseball cap long enough to run her fingers through her hair. "Want to stay and watch the rest of the shoot?"

He smiled. "I wish I could, but I can't," he said, openly regretful. "I've got an appointment across town in half an hour."

"Too bad," she said with a grin. "You might have enjoyed it."

"I'm sure I would have," he agreed. "Can I have a rain check?"

"Of course." She paused. "I've got one coming up—a hot-air balloon in Central Park."

He chuckled. "Sounds like fun."

"Oh, I'm sure it will be," she said. "Ever been in one?"

"A hot air balloon?" Mitch shook his head. "No, I can't say that I have."

"There's nothing else in the world like it," she told him. "I once took a balloon flight across Kenya on a vacation adventure, and believe me, it *was* an adventure!"

"You like adventure, don't you?" he asked.

She cocked her head to one side, regarding him with open amusement. "What makes you say that?" she asked.

"It's true, isn't it?"

"Sure it's true," she said with a nod, "but what makes you say so?"

Mitch shrugged. "I don't know," he said thoughtfully. "You just strike me as the type of person who needs constant stimulation, that's all."

She raised an eyebrow. "Oh?"

"I didn't mean it that way," he said quickly. "I only meant that you seem to me to be the adventurous type."

She nodded, deciding to let him off the hook. "True enough," she said. "Never a dull moment, that's my motto."

"About dinner," he said then, abruptly changing the subject. "Do you have any preferences? French? Italian?"

She winked playfully. "I'll try anything once," she told him.

And she meant it. In more ways than one.

She was still thinking about it when she returned to her studio late that afternoon. She'd come on to him today, as she'd wanted to from the day she met him.

And he had responded.

I wasn't imagining it, she told herself. The chemistry between us is genuine. We click.

That was one way of putting it, anyway.

If only he could see it. Or did he already?

She busied herself in the darkroom for the next few hours, developing the film she'd shot that day.

That, and thinking about her conversation with Mitch. What, she asked herself now, did she expect from him, from their relationship, such as it was? What did she feel for him? What *could* she feel for him?

He's one good-looking guy, she thought now. He just needs to loosen up, learn to live a little.

Well, at least he came to the right teacher.

This was going to be interesting—very interesting, indeed. They were as unlike as any two people could possibly be. Oil and water, day and night, champagne and beer nuts. They couldn't get odds in Vegas on their relationship even developing, let alone progressing to a first date.

I should have put money on it, she decided.

As she checked the film she'd developed, she noticed that she'd caught Mitch in the background in one shot, apparently when he first arrived on the observation deck. She studied it for a moment. He *could* be a model, she decided. The camera definitely loves him.

Could *she* love him?

Where is this coming from? she asked herself. Why am I asking myself these questions?

Why does it matter?

"Danny?" a female voice called out to her from the studio.

She recognized it immediately. "I'm in the darkroom, Phoebe," she called back.

"What? I can't hear you!" She was getting closer.

"I said I'm in the darkroom. Don't open the door!" Danny shouted, certain that at any moment she would do just that. Phoebe was a first-class rep, but sometimes she could be a real airhead, usually at the worst possible times.

"I wasn't about to," Phoebe assured her. She was up against the door now.

"What's up?" Danny wanted to know.

"Nothing special," Phoebe said. "I just had a meeting downtown, and since I was almost in the neighborhood—"

"You thought you'd drop by," Danny finished. Typical Phoebe. Dropping by was one of Phoebe's favorite activities. She almost never called first. Unlike the cavalry, Phoebe never warned her targets.

It made Danny wonder sometimes how she fared with the editors and advertisers she did business with.

"Well, yeah."

"You're in luck," Danny told her. "I'm just finishing up here, then I'm all yours."

Phoebe hooted with laughter. "All mine?" she asked. "I don't think so."

Finally finished, Danny stuck her head through the door. "Now what do you mean by that?" she questioned.

"Only that if you were going to give yourself to anybody, my money would be on that good-looking P.I. you hired," Phoebe said, adjusting the wide-brimmed hat she wore.

"Don't start," Danny warned.

"I'm not the one who's starting," Phoebe pointed out.

"No?"

"No!"

"I hear he paid you a visit at the shoot today," Phoebe said.

Danny laughed. "Your spies really are everywhere, aren't they?"

"Just about," Phoebe answered without hesitation. "Want to fill me in?"

"Not really," Danny told her. "Didn't your spies give you any details?"

"None of them were close enough to eavesdrop," Phoebe lamented.

"Then they didn't tell you we're running away together?" Danny asked, deciding this was as good a time as any to have some fun with Phoebe. "Or that we plan to live naked on a sun-baked Greek island?"

"Be serious!" Phoebe snorted.

Danny raised an eyebrow. "What makes you think I'm not?" she asked.

"Knowing you, it's possible—anything's possible—but I doubt it," Phoebe told her.

Danny laughed. "If you must know, I'm having dinner with him."

"Tonight?"

"That's the plan, yes," Danny said with a nod.

"Where?"

"As if I'd tell you!" Danny howled gleefully.

"Why not?"

"Because adventurous as I am, I don't want to get acquainted with him in front of a live audience," Danny said.

"Would I follow you to a restaurant?" Phoebe asked, feigning hurt feelings.

"You'd follow me to the moon if you thought it would produce some decent gossip!" Danny laughed.

"Seriously, what *are* your plans?" Phoebe pressed.

"Seriously, I'm not going to tell you," Danny insisted.

Phoebe studied her for a moment. "You really care for this guy, don't you?" she asked finally.

"It's too soon to know what I do or don't feel for him," Danny responded. "I think I like him. I know I'm attracted to him. But beyond that—" she shrugged "—who knows?"

"Well, if he's what you want, I hope you get him," Phoebe told her.

Danny laughed. "You make him sound like an assignment!"

"Approach it any way you choose," Phoebe advised her. "You will anyway."

"That's your problem," Danny told her.

"What?"

"You need a man, Phoebe, in the worst kind of way," Danny diagnosed.

Phoebe winced. "An unfortunate choice of words," she declared.

"But very true."

"I think I'll invoke the Fifth Amendment," Phoebe responded.

"A wise decision," Danny told her. "Any attempt at a real answer would definitely prove incriminating."

"To say the least."

"I could always fix you up," Danny offered.

"Nooo, thank you!" Phoebe waved her off. "To say that you and I don't go for the same kind of men is like saying Republicans and Democrats don't see eye to eye."

Danny didn't respond. She wasn't thinking about men, plural. She was only thinking about one man at the moment.

Mitch Newman.

Chapter Four

"**Y**ou're full of surprises," Danny told him.

Now, sitting across from her at a table at Scarlatti, an Italian restaurant on East Fifty-second Street near Madison Avenue, Mitch found he'd surprised himself.

Probably more than I surprised her, he thought.

It had been a while since the last time Mitch had eaten at Scarlatti—though he noticed Danny was on a first-name basis with most of the restaurant's staff. She obviously knew her way around the formal, peach-colored dining room.

They were anything *but* formal with her.

"I'll have the messaluna ravioli," she told the waiter who'd come to take their order. "Mitch?"

"What—oh!" He quickly scanned the menu he was still holding. "I think I'll have the sea bass." It was roasted with herbs and considered one of the best dishes on the menu.

"You like to play it safe, don't you?" Danny observed.

He nodded. "Most of the time, yes," he admitted.

"A pity."

"Why do you say that?"

She smiled. An incredible smile, indeed. "If you always stick with what you know, you never experience anything new. You never know what you might be missing."

He smiled, too. "Point well taken."

As the waiter headed back to the kitchen, Danny turned to Mitch again. "Are you sure this isn't a business meeting?" she wanted to know.

"I often meet with clients outside the office," he explained.

"Of course," Danny said with a knowing smile.

"I think it's sometimes easier for the client to relax and recall things they might not remember in the more formal office atmosphere," he went on.

"I'm sure that's true of some people," Danny agreed with a nod.

She was still smiling.

She's enjoying this, Mitch thought. She's not buying my lame excuses at all. "But not you?"

"Hardly."

"Why does that not surprise me?" he wondered aloud.

"So, why are we here?" she asked.

"I just told you."

Danny was openly amused. "That doesn't exactly apply to my case, Mitch," she pointed out.

"You don't think so?"

"No," she said. "There's nothing for me to remember, relaxed or otherwise. Someone left me a lot of money. I don't know who—or why. I hired you to find out. It's that simple."

He shook his head. "It's never that simple," he said.

"No?"

"Not by a long shot," he told her. "Whoever left it to you did so for a reason. No one ever does this sort of thing randomly."

"Obviously not."

"So probing your background is one of the ways we come up with the identities of people who might have been both able and willing to leave you that kind of money."

"I see," she said.

Mitch was sure that she did.

"I've given this a lot of thought—" he started.

"So have I," she said, cutting him off, "and I can't think of anyone—not a single, solitary soul— who had that kind of money, died recently and would leave it to me."

The bottom line, however, was that someone had.

"We have to be missing something," he maintained.

"I don't know what it would be," she said, shaking her head. "How many times have we beat this dead horse, anyway?"

Dead horse?

"Not enough, obviously."

"I'm telling you now that it would be a waste of time," Danny insisted. "There's no one."

Not even an old boyfriend? Mitch wondered. Looking at her now, he was reminded once again that this was a woman men noticed, a woman men wanted. She was the kind of woman a man never forgot.

Just the thought of the men in Danny's life made Mitch miserable.

Maybe one of them wanted to make sure she never forgot him.

That theory doesn't hold water, he told himself. If one of her former loves wanted to make sure she remembered him, he wouldn't have gone to such extraordinary lengths to keep his identity a secret.

"What about former lovers?" he asked.

Bad choice of words, you idiot, he mentally reprimanded himself.

She couldn't hide her surprise. "What?"

"Have you thought about it?" he asked.

Or them?

Any of them?

At all?

"Not really," she admitted, shaking her head.

"Think about it."

"Come on, Mitch—" she began.

"Danny, you're a very attractive woman," he said. "There must have been a lot of men in your life."

"Now, wait a minute!"

Bad move, Newman, he told himself.

You've made her mad.

Great.

"I'm not insulting you," he said quickly. "Actually, it could be considered a compliment."

"It doesn't sound like one to me," she said somewhat defensively.

"You're not going to convince me you're the wallflower type," he said.

"I'm not going to try," she shot back at him.

"I'm not accusing you of anything," he insisted, lowering his voice. "I'm only saying maybe someone you had a relationship with in the past still had serious feelings for you and wanted to leave you something to prove it."

Danny thought about it for a moment. "If that were the case," she said carefully, "why would he keep his identity a secret?"

"I can think of a number of reasons," he told her.

But no valid ones, he was thinking.

Only one of his theories made any sense at all.

*   *   *

He couldn't leave things like that between them; he
had to see her right away, so the next day he went to
see her at work.

She wasn't shooting in the studio that morning,
however. When he called, he was told she was doing
the photography for a hairspray ad on a yacht in New
York Harbor. She'd picked a less than ideal day for
it, he decided as he got out of his car and headed for
the pier. The sky looked threatening; storms were
predicted for the afternoon. Then he smiled to himself. It would take more than a storm to scare Danny
off. She'd probably photographed hurricanes.

She was surprised to see him, however. "What are
you doing here?" she asked, handing one of her assistants a camera to be reloaded.

"I would ask you the same question," he said with
a grin. "In case you haven't noticed, bad weather is
approaching."

"I've noticed," she assured him. "I don't have a
choice. The magazine has a deadline."

"I see. What happens if the rain comes before
you're finished?" he wanted to know.

"We take shelter and wait for it to pass." She took
the reloaded camera. "Want to stick around and see
who wins—me or Mother Nature?"

He laughed at the image that conjured up. "My
money's on you," he told her.

She gave him a dubious smile. "As much as I do
appreciate the vote of confidence, that remains to be
seen," she said.

"We'll see."

"Right." She was amused, but it was obvious she wasn't the least bit nervous.

"I need to talk to you," he said then, lowering his voice.

"About what?"

"Business."

"In that case, you'll have to stick around," she said. "I can't take a break until I'm finished—not with this storm coming."

He nodded. "All right," he agreed. It didn't exactly come as a surprise.

She had an assistant find a chair for him that would give him a bird's-eye view of the models. They were three of the most beautiful women in the business, but he was staring at Danny.

Smooth sailing it wasn't, even though they never left the dock. Even in the harbor, the impending storm made the waters dark and choppy. It wasn't long before Mitch began to feel a little queasy. Then a *lot* queasy.

Danny was amused. "What's the matter, Newman?" she asked. "Can't hack it?"

"I'll be all right," he insisted.

Then he threw up.

Danny did what she'd said she couldn't do—she stopped the shoot. "I've got to take him home," she told her assistant. "I'll be back."

"Before the storm hits?"

Danny frowned. "I'll have to be."

But she wasn't.

It started to rain as she parked her minivan in front of Mitch's building. "Great," she grumbled, helping him inside. "What else can go wrong?"

There was a loud rumble of thunder.

She rolled her eyes skyward. "I had to ask," she groaned.

By the time they got into his apartment, the downpour could be seen from the large windows in his living room. "Sorry about your shoot," he said in a weak voice.

"Don't be," she said, holding him up. "We would have been rained out anyway." She looked around. "Which way is the bedroom?"

He gestured.

She led him into the bedroom and helped him lie down. She pulled his shoes off and unbuttoned his shirt. Then she went into the adjoining bathroom and got a damp washcloth. When she returned, she wiped his face and neck. "Better not to eat anything for a while," she told him. "But if you want anything to drink—"

He shook his head. "Not now."

She nodded. "I'll stick around until you're feeling better," she said, "just in case you need anything."

He wanted to say, "I need *you*," but didn't. Instead he said, "Thanks for staying."

She nodded. "You'd have done the same for me."

You have no idea, he thought.

"Maybe you should try to get some sleep," she suggested.

"Maybe."

He did doze off for a little while. When he woke, she was sitting in a chair near his bed, reading. She smiled when she saw he was awake. "Feeling any better?" she wanted to know.

"A little."

She put down the book. "Hungry yet?" she asked.

"A little," he repeated.

"I made some soup, just in case."

He raised an eyebrow. "*You* made it?"

She made a face. "Don't look so impressed," she told him. "It came from a can."

"Not a gourmet chef?" he asked. "I'm disillusioned."

"Ah, you *are* feeling better!" She laughed. "Do you want the soup or not?"

"I'll take a chance on it."

"You mean since it came from a can."

"At least I know what I'm getting," he pointed out.

"You sure about that?" she asked with an evil smile.

He was still smiling when she left the room to get the soup. It had been worth getting seasick just to have her come here and take care of him. He didn't care if she could cook or not. To him she was perfect just the way she was.

Though it probably wouldn't do to tell *her* that.

Chapter Five

Something was wrong here.

Something was definitely wrong, Mitch concluded as he searched the microfiche birth records at the Department of Vital Statistics in Albany, New York, a few days later.

There was no record of Danny's birth. Anywhere. Not in Albany, anyway. Didn't she tell him all the Vine children had been born here?

I don't believe this, Mitch thought, frustrated. Everywhere I turn, I hit a roadblock.

Every time I come up with what seems like a lead, it only leads to another complication. Fishy, to say the least.

This was the most puzzling complication to date.

He'd been over everything at least three times in the past two days. There was no mistake. Nothing had been missed, nothing overlooked. There was no record of the birth of Danielle Vine to Harris and Millicent Vine. All of their other children were on the record here, but not Danny.

Not that Mitch was all that surprised.

Almost from the beginning, he'd suspected that her parents had something to do with all of this. At the very least, they were hiding something.

But what?

Was it possible that Danny wasn't really their daughter? he wondered. Could she have been adopted? He'd wondered about that the first time he met with her, but had initially dismissed the idea because he felt it would have been impossible to keep such a secret in so large a family.

If Danny had been the eldest child, maybe. But she was the youngest. The older children would have known the difference.

How could they have possibly kept such a secret? he wondered.

They would have known their parents had brought home a baby without their mother being pregnant.

Danny would have known, because someone would have told her. Kids talk, he told himself, especially when they're not supposed to.

Still . . .

It was the only explanation that made sense, he concluded as he wrapped up at the hall of records and headed back to his hotel. Someone had left Danny an enormous amount of money. The kind of money one only left to a blood relative. There was no record of her birth where there should have been a record. Danny admitted her parents had a peculiar response to the news of her inheritance.

Two and two usually equaled four, didn't it?

Yes, it did, except where Danny Vine was concerned, he decided. Nothing about her case made sense.

All the other records *had* been there—the marriage of Harris and Millicent Vine, the births of Camille, Michael, Eugene, Nicholas, Meryl, Karyn, Sally and Christiane Vine.

But not Danny.

Why? he wondered again.

Mitch could think of only one reason why it wouldn't be.

He hoped he was wrong.

For Danny's sake, he hoped he was wrong. If he was right, she clearly didn't know she was adopted. How would she take the news?

The more he thought about it, the more certain he was that he had to approach the subject again with Danny, and he dreaded it. He knew how she was going to react—exactly the same way she'd reacted the last time he brought it up. She was adamant that her parents couldn't possibly be hiding anything of any importance.

Her faith in them was unshakable.

He could only hope it wasn't misplaced.

He had to admit, if only to himself, that he was in danger of losing his objectivity. If this were any other case, he wouldn't hesitate to tell the client what he'd found, what he suspected. He resisted telling Danny, not for professional reasons but for personal reasons. He knew she would be angry. She might even fire him.

That was what bothered him most. If she fired him, if she called off the investigation, he might never see her again.

He wasn't ready to risk that.

Get a grip on yourself, Newman, he thought angrily. This is your job. No matter what you feel for her, you have an obligation to her to do the job she hired you to do.

Feel for her?

Did those words come from him? They'd taken him by surprise, since until this moment he hadn't even acknowledged the possibility that he might actually have feelings for her.

He'd been attracted to her right from the beginning, but that wasn't the same thing as having feelings for her, was it?

He didn't have a clue.

This was an area in which he had practically no experience. *Feelings* . . . He frowned. Might as well have been some foreign language as far as he was concerned. A language he'd never quite had an ear for.

Sort of like a country I've never visited, he thought miserably.

Or another planet.

He checked out of the motel early in the morning and stopped at a local Shoney's for breakfast before starting the long drive back to Manhattan. En route, he placed a call to Danny on his car phone.

I have to face her sooner or later, he decided.

One of her assistants answered. "Divine Studios."

Mitch smiled to himself. That name was perfect—for her and for her studio. "Is Danny there?" he asked.

"Who's calling, please?"

"Mitch Newman."

"Just a minute."

A few moments later, Danny came on the line. "Hi, Mitch. What's up?" she asked, her tone cheerful.

"I need to see you," he said, getting right to the point.

She laughed. "I'm flattered."

"I'm serious, Danny."

"So am I," she assured him.

"Danny..."

There was only a brief hesitation. "You've found something?"

"You might say that."

"Good or bad?"

He hesitated. This wasn't something he wanted to discuss with her over the phone.

"I think I'd rather tell you about it when I see you." Might as well face her wrath in person, he decided. "Can you meet me at my office?"

"What time?" she asked.

He glanced at his watch. "Around noon?"

"Noon? In that case, let's discuss it over lunch," she suggested.

"Where?"

"Do you like Mexican?"

"It's one of my favorites."

"Great," she said. "Do you know El Teddy's on west Broadway?

"Yeah."

"Meet me there at noon."

"I'll see you there."

Danny was still thinking about that conversation as she sat at a table at El Teddy's, waiting for Mitch to arrive. This was one of her favorite restaurants, and normally she never tired of its offbeat interior—she loved the glitter and tile—but today she was oblivious to it.

Why did Mitch want to see her?

He'd sounded so mysterious on the phone. He wouldn't tell her where he was or what he'd been doing or what he'd found.

Why?

It had to be bad news. Bad news always came in person.

She checked the time. Mitch was fifteen minutes late. Not like him at all. He was normally so punctual. Where is he? she wondered anxiously.

And what did he find out?

This was making her nuts.

He wasn't calling from Manhattan, she was fairly certain of that. He hadn't said anything to her, specifically or otherwise, to indicate that he'd left the city in search of answers, but she had a strong feeling that this was exactly what he'd done.

What did he find? she wondered again.

"Danny?"

She looked up as Mitch approached her table. "I was beginning to wonder about you," she told him as he sat down.

"I got caught in traffic—there was a four-car pileup." He signaled their waiter. "I need a drink," he told her.

She nodded. Tell me! Tell me! her mind shouted. Don't keep me in suspense.

"It was a mess," he said.

"What?"

"The accident. I was stuck there almost an hour."

"Where?"

"About two miles south of Albany," he told her.

"Albany?" So he had been away. "What were you doing in Albany?"

"I was at the Department of Vital Statistics," he told her, pausing to tell the waiter what he wanted to drink. He turned back to Danny. "Have you ordered yet?"

Danny shook her head.

"Are you ready to?"

She forced a smile. "As ready as I'll ever be." She looked up at the waiter. "I'll have the cactus salad with jicama."

The waiter turned to Mitch.

"I'll have the *masa* tart," he said.

After the waiter had gone, Danny turned back to Mitch. "What were you looking for at the Department of Vital Statistics?" she asked.

"Your birth certificate," he answered honestly.

She laughed. "You didn't have to go to all that trouble," she told him. "All you had to do was ask me to see it."

"As I recall, that was a sore subject with you," he reminded her.

"Not at all," she insisted. "I'd be more than happy to show you anything that will prove you're off base about my parents."

"Will it?" he asked.

She shot him a wary look. "You're not going to start that again, are you?" she asked.

"Danny, there's no record of your birth," he said. "Not in Albany, anyway."

"Impossible!"

"It's not there," he insisted. "Believe me, I looked. I found your parents' marriage license and the birth certificates of all of your siblings—but not yours."

"That can't be," she said, shaking her head. It just wasn't possible. It wasn't.

"I'm telling you, Danny, it's not there," he told her again. Then, after a brief pause, he asked, "Is it possible you could have been born somewhere else?"

She thought about it. "I don't know," she said finally. "I suppose it could be."

There had to be an explanation.

"The place of birth would be on your birth certificate," he reminded her. "If you have it—"

"I've never really looked at it," she admitted. "I used it to get my driver's license and my passport. Other than that, it stays in my safety deposit box."

He probably didn't believe her, but it was the truth. That sort of thing had never mattered all that much to her. She knew who she was; she didn't need a piece of paper to verify it for her.

"You've never even examined it?" he asked, surprised.

Danny shook her head. "No—never had any reason to," she told him.

"Really."

The waiter interrupted them then, bringing their lunch. Neither of them spoke again until he had gone.

"You don't believe me, do you?" Danny asked.

He shook his head. "I didn't say that."

"You didn't have to."

"Didn't your parents ever mention where you were born?" he asked.

"Not that I can recall." Danny's smile was weak. "I guess after nine kids, the little details become less and less important." She was still convinced there had to be an acceptable explanation.

She was sure of it.

"Maybe," he acknowledged with a nod.

But Danny had the feeling he wasn't at all convinced.

Chapter Six

He has to be wrong.

He has to be, Danny thought as she let herself into her apartment that evening, still puzzled by what Mitch had found—or rather *didn't* find—in Albany. It didn't make sense. None of this made any sense. He probably didn't believe her when she said she'd never really given much thought to her birth certificate, but it was the truth. She knew when and where she was born—or at least she'd always thought she knew, until now.

She'd never really had any need to pay too much attention to it. Even when she got her driver's license, her father had been there, and he'd brought her birth certificate along. He'd gotten her passport, too, come to think of it. No! She immediately pushed the thought from her mind. She was starting to think like Mitch. She knew what he was thinking, and he was wrong.

There had to be a logical explanation. She was sure of it.

Her parents could explain it, but unfortunately they were away for the weekend. They'd gone to visit friends in Boston. Her mother grew up there, and most of her family and childhood friends still lived there.

Camille. That's it, she thought. Camille was older than Danny by twelve years. Her eldest sister would know. She'd often mentioned things she remembered about their mother's pregnancy with Danny and what Danny herself had been like as a baby. She dropped her oversize shoulder bag on the overstuffed couch, kicked off her shoes and went to the phone to call her.

The housekeeper picked up on the third ring. "Edwards residence," she said with a clear, if a bit too formal, New England accent.

"Martha, this is Danny Vine," she identified herself, removing one large, dangling earring as she put the receiver closer to her ear. "Is Camille there?"

"I'm sorry, Miss Vine, Mr. and Mrs. Edwards are vacationing in Italy," Martha told her apologetically. "They won't be back until the twenty-fifth."

"They've left already?" Danny slapped her forehead. She'd almost forgotten, even though all Camille had talked about for the past six months was the extended vacation she and her family would be spending in Italy—Rome, Venice, Milan, Portofino. "I thought they were leaving next week!"

"They left yesterday," Martha informed her. "But they will be calling in from time to time. Shall I give them a message?" she offered.

"No, that's all right, but thanks anyway." Danny sighed. She didn't expect her sister to call her from Italy just to answer what was probably going to sound like a stupid question to start with. "I'll talk to her when she gets back."

"I'll tell her you called."

"Fine. Do that."

She hung up slowly, feeling as if the wind had been knocked out of her sails and unsure of which way to turn next. "Great," she said with a heavy sigh. Camille and Paul were in Italy. Her parents were in Boston. Who else in the family would know? Her brothers? Maybe, but the odds were against finding them—any of them—home on a Friday night. She smiled wearily. Couldn't get odds on that in Vegas, she told herself. She'd be more likely to find them at one of their favorite local haunts—or even the police station.

She decided to call Sally. It was probably going to prove to be a waste of time.

But then, a long shot was better than none at all.

Sally was home, but wasn't able to tell Danny what she needed to know. "I was there, sure, but I was only two years old," Sally reminded her. As if Danny needed to be reminded. I had to try, she told herself.

"So you don't remember?"

Sally laughed. "Hardly." Then she asked, "Have you talked to any of the Three Stooges?"

"On a Friday night?" Danny asked. "I'd have a better shot at getting the White House on the line!"

"True," Sally conceded. Their brothers' reputation as world-class party animals was well-deserved.

Later that evening, over a dinner of salad and fresh fruit from the corner deli, Danny pored over all the old family photographs in her possession. She'd started taking pictures at a very early age—as soon as she was able to hold a camera. She still had every photo she'd taken over the years, as well as some old family photos her parents had given her to encourage her early interest in photography. There weren't all that many—her parents still had most of them— and those she did have didn't provide any clues to whether or not she'd been born in Troy.

Thinking about it now, she wasn't sure what she expected to find. "A waste of time," she proclaimed. "Why did I think this was going to accomplish anything?"

Among the old photographs she did have, she found one of her mother holding her—she couldn't have been more than a couple of weeks old—with Sally, Meryl, and Christiane looking on. There were also a number of her own baby photos.

And maybe a half dozen of her very pregnant mother, taken in the weeks before her birth.

Danny was excited. This was just what she'd been looking for. This was proof positive that her mother was really her mother. She couldn't wait to show Mitch, to prove he was wrong. Her parents had nothing to hide.

Mitch is wrong, she told herself. He has to be.

"Right in here, Ms. Vine."

The bank manager stepped aside, allowing Danny to enter the small, windowless room within the vault. He removed her safety deposit box from the wall of boxes and placed it on the small table in the center of the room. "I'll be back when you're finished," he told her.

She nodded. "Thank you," she responded quietly.

After he was gone, she took her key from her pocket and opened the box. With a heavy sigh, she began her slow, deliberate examination of its contents: some stocks given her by her parents...her passport, which she hadn't looked at since her trip to Egypt last year...college and high school diplomas...some of the jewelry her mother gave her from her own collection. Danny kept it because it had been her mother's and she was sentimental about it, but she rarely wore it. Too expensive. Danny leaned toward unusual costume pieces herself.

She picked up her birth certificate and studied it for a moment, surprised to find it gave her place of birth as New York City. She'd never noticed that before—or maybe she had and just never gave it much thought. That sort of thing didn't matter to her.

Until now, anyway.

She wished she knew where Mitch Newman was coming from. How could he even suggest the Vines might not really be her parents? If she were adopted, she'd know it! Her parents wouldn't have kept anything, certainly not anything so important, from her.

Never.

She wished she knew where he was coming from, period. There were times she thought he was really interested in her—as a woman as well as a client—but there were other times she wondered if he even saw her as a woman.

She certainly saw him as a man.

Time will tell, she told herself as she put everything but her birth certificate back in the box and called for the bank manager to have a photocopy made.

"I have a copy of my birth certificate—just to put your suspicious mind at ease," Danny told Mitch as she unlocked her front door.

"I didn't say—" he began.

"Yes, you did," she retorted, not giving him a chance to protest. "You suggested my parents hadn't been completely honest with me."

"I didn't say they had lied to you. I merely asked if it were possible they might not have told you everything," he maintained.

"Right." She opened the door, flipping the switch just inside that turned on the lights in the living room. He entered the apartment behind her and closed the door. "Can I get you anything to drink?"

He shook his head. "I'm fine."

She nodded. "Okay." She took an envelope from the small antique desk in one corner of the room and handed it to him as he sat down on the couch. He didn't open it right away. He was taking in his surroundings, learning things he didn't already know about Danny Vine from her environment, things he didn't know but still was not surprised by.

She didn't use a decorator, he was sure of that. Everything in this room reflected Danny's personality. Every item, every piece of furniture had her personal stamp on it, from the eclectic mix of antiques and modern furniture to the incredibly comfortable overstuffed sofa, to the odd assortment of animal figurines, to the unique items no doubt collected in the course of her travels that now adorned her walls.

Pure Danny, he thought with mild amusement.

"Aren't you going to look at it?"

He looked up. Danny was standing in front of him, watching him expectantly.

"Oh—yeah," he said, looking at the envelope in his hand again. He opened it and removed the photocopy inside. Her birth certificate. Nothing out of the ordinary except the place of birth.

He looked up at her again. "New York City?"

She nodded, grinning. "I'd never really looked at it, and I can't remember Mom or Dad every mentioning it," she said. "I just assumed, I guess, that I was born in Troy like everybody else."

He raised an eyebrow. "Everybody else?"

She made a face. "You know what I mean."

He smiled. "Yeah."

"I guess that proves you were off base."

"Maybe."

She stared at him incredulously. "Maybe?"

"It's still possible," he pointed out.

She rolled her eyes skyward, exasperated. "No, it's not," she insisted.

"Okay, okay, have it your way," he said quickly. "If you have another answer, I'm willing to listen."

"I don't," she reluctantly conceded, "but there has to be one—and you have to find it."

He didn't respond. He got to his feet and crossed the room to the bookshelves to have a closer look at the numerous framed photos there. Photos of Danny's family—parents, brothers, sisters.

"That's Mom and Dad on their most recent anniversary," she told him as he picked up one of the photos. "And the one next to it is the Three Stooges."

He grinned. "Three Stooges?"

She nodded. "My brothers, the triplets—Gene, Nick and Mike."

He reached for another frame. "And this one?"

"My sisters, Sally and Meryl," she said. "Over there are Karyn and Camille, and the dramatic-looking lady is Christiane."

"An actress," he guessed.

She smiled. "Very perceptive."

He turned to study her for a moment. "You don't look like any of them," he said finally.

She gave an offhand shrug that said she knew it but didn't think it was such a big deal. "Dad says I look like his great-grandmother. Mom says I don't look like anyone else on the face of the earth."

That was the understatement of the year, he thought but didn't say.

It was at that moment that he realized their faces were only inches apart and getting even closer as Danny leaned forward to replace one of the frames.

Suddenly, without warning, she kissed him.

It was a quick, playful kiss, but a kiss nonetheless. He felt his heart beating wildly against the wall of his chest as she withdrew and gave him the sexiest smile he'd ever been on the receiving end of.

"Gotcha," she said in a low, sexy voice.

He managed a smile. "You sure did."

"You don't care much for surprises, do you?" she asked.

"Not really," he admitted.

"Too bad," she told him. "Always knowing what to expect sort of takes the fun out of life, don't you think?"

"No danger of that with you around," he said.

"I'll take that as a compliment," she said.

She would.

"Mickey's late!" Danny announced impatiently to all within earshot.

Normally, Danny was not difficult to work with. She was, however, a perfectionist. She didn't tolerate sloppy work or tardiness. Even a lapse in professionalism made her crazy. She expected everyone she worked with, from the models to her own assistants, to be on time, prepared and willing to do a shot over and over again until it was done right.

"Mickey's not coming," one of her assistants told her.

"What do you mean, he's not coming?" she demanded.

"Just that. He's sick."

"He'd better be *dead!*" Danny snapped crossly. "Why wasn't I told sooner?"

"His agent just called," the assistant explained. "It's stomach flu or something like that."

"They could have let us know yesterday!"

"Apparently not," the assistant said, shaking her head. "He was fine yesterday. This morning, he's spending most of his time with his head in the toilet."

"Great. Has anything been done to get me a replacement?"

The assistant shrugged. "The agency's trying, that's all I know."

Just as Danny was about to call it off, she spotted the answer to her problem. Mitch was emerging from the elevators, coming toward her. He was grinning.

"Just the person I've been waiting for!" she called out to him.

"Not possible," he told her. "You didn't know I was coming."

"Maybe not, but you couldn't have come at a better time," she assured him, putting one arm around him.

"Oh?"

"My male model called in sick."

"What's that got to do with—" He stopped short. "Now wait a minute—if you're saying what I think you're saying—"

She nodded. "I am."

He shook his head emphatically. "No way!"

"Oh, come on, Mitch," she said, pleading. "You'd be great."

"No, I wouldn't," he argued. "I'm not a model, Danny. I don't even like having my picture taken."

"That's hard to believe," she responded in a disbelieving tone. "You're a good-looking man, Mitch Newman. I'll bet the camera loves you."

"Well, I don't love *it*," he insisted stubbornly.

"You'd be doing me a big favor."

"And making a fool of myself in the process."

"You might be surprised."

"I'm sure."

"I'll take you out to dinner afterward," she promised.

Reluctantly, he reconsidered. It might not be *too* bad—and he did want to help her out. "All right," he surrendered.

She brightened immediately. "Great. You can change in there," she said, pointing toward the makeshift dressing room.

"Change? Into what?"

"The trunks, of course."

"Trunks?"

"Sure," she said with a nod. "This is a swimsuit ad."

"You should have told me that before I agreed to do it."

"Would it have made a difference?"

"You'd better believe it!"

"Why?"

"There's no way I'm posing for an ad in a national magazine in trunks."

Danny thought about it for a moment. "Tell you what," she said finally. "Let me shoot the photos. I'll let you see them when I develop them, and if you're not pleasantly surprised, I won't use them. Deal?"

He gave it some thought. "Deal."

He changed into the trunks, a surprisingly good fit—he and the missing model were almost the same size—and emerged from the dressing room. "You look great," Danny assured him.

"Sure."

"You do," she insisted. "I wouldn't use you if you didn't, believe me."

"Where do you want me?" he asked.

She found his self-consciousness a refreshing change from the vain models she was accustomed to working with. "Over there," she said, gesturing toward the large, brightly colored beach umbrellas strategically placed by her assistants.

She gave him instructions as to how she wanted him to pose.

"Treat the camera like a lover," she urged. "Smile for it, seduce it."

"Easy for you to say," he grumbled.

Things went more smoothly than either of them expected, once he overcame his initial nervousness. "You're a natural," she told him when they were finished. "You should think about doing this for a living."

He laughed at the thought. "No way!"

"You'd be good at it," she predicted. "You'd make a lot of money."

"Not for any amount of money would I ever consider doing this every day," he insisted. "I pity the models who do."

"Don't," she told him. "They work hard, but some of them couldn't live without the camera's love."

"They must be nuts."

"Sometimes, yes."

"They'd have to be."

"You're sure you wouldn't want to do this again."

"Absolutely. Now, about dinner..."

"Is he in?"

Mitch's secretary looked up from the ten talons to which she'd been applying tomato red polish. She seemed to look Danny up and down. "Yeah, he's in there, but I think he's on the phone." The woman stared intently at Danny, which made her uncomfortable to a degree that she almost never was.

"Is something wrong?" Or are you just weird? Danny wondered. She welcomed this kind of attention from the opposite sex, but certainly not from other women!

"I'm just curious, that's all," Shirley told her, still obviously fascinated.

Danny gave her a quizzical look. "About what?"

"You," Shirley answered honestly. "I've wondered for a long time now what kind of woman turned him on."

"Him?" Danny asked, puzzled.

"Mitch," Shirley stated in a way that made it clear she was surprised by having to clarify the obvious.

Danny smiled. If only she could believe that. There were times—most of the time, actually—she wasn't sure Mitch was even willing to acknowledge she was alive, except as a client.

In spite of my best efforts, she thought wryly.

Aloud she said, "I think you're probably mistaken—"

"Not where Mitch is concerned," Shirley assured her, waving one hand dismissively. Or was she just drying her nails? "I've worked for him too long. I know him too well. He's got it bad for you." She spoke with absolute certainty.

Before Danny could respond, the door opened and Mitch emerged from his office. He is one good-looking man, Danny thought, looking at him now. If Shirley was telling the truth...well, who knew what might happen when all of this was over.

She'd certainly welcome that idea.

What about him?

"Danny," he said, genuinely surprised to see her. "What brings you here?"

"I have something to show you," she told him. "I think it might clear up a few things you've been wondering about."

He raised an eyebrow. "In that case, come on in," he said, gesturing toward his private office as he dropped some papers on top of the pile already waiting in Shirley's In tray. He looked at the secretary and winked.

Danny saw Shirley wink back at him.

What, she found herself wondering, are those two up to?

And what does it have to do with me?

He held the door for her, then followed her inside and closed the door. "Now, what is it you want to show me?" he asked as he strode around the desk and seated himself. He leaned back in his chair and regarded her with mild amusement.

Enjoy it while you can, Newman, Danny thought.

"Proof," she told him, enjoying his initial response.

"Proof? Of what?" It was gratifying to see him sit up and take notice of something other than her legs.

"Proof that your theory about my parents not really being my parents is way off base," she said smugly. She was going to enjoy hearing him say he was wrong. A humble hunk. She rather liked the sound of that. Reaching into her bag, she took out an envelope and passed it across the desk to him.

"What's this?"

"See for yourself," she suggested. She couldn't wait.

He nodded and opened the envelope, removing the old photos. He examined them one by one. "A very pregnant woman," he commented.

"My mother," she told him. "Look at the date on the back."

He did.

"They were taken just before I was born," Danny explained. "You'll notice that *my mother* is the one who's quite pregnant.'' Let's see him explain that away.

"No doubt about that," Mitch said, nodding his agreement.

"Now will you admit you were wrong?" Danny asked. C'mon, Mitch, she thought. Let's hear "uncle"—loud and clear.

"Hmm?" He continued to study the photographs. "About what?"

"About my parents not really being my parents," she said as he put the photographs back in the envelope and returned it to her.

Their eyes met and held for a long moment. There were sparks—yes, definitely sparks—but as always happened, one or both of them moved to extinguish those sparks before they could ignite.

Why? she found herself wondering.

"I never said that, exactly—" he began.

"You suggested it!" she reminded him, unwilling to let him off the hook so easily.

"You should have become a lawyer, Danny," he said, chuckling. "You do like to argue."

Stop avoiding the issue, she thought. You're good at that.

"You were wrong, Mitch." Why won't you admit it?

He nodded. "I was wrong—about that," he conceded. "But something is wrong, Danny. There's no record of your birth in Albany. Someone has bequeathed you a rather large sum of money. It doesn't add up." Clearly, something about this *still* bothered him.

Why?

"What are you saying?" Danny asked carefully.

"It's like a puzzle with several pieces missing," he said, openly perplexed. "Obviously your mother is your biological mother, but there are still unanswered questions."

"So how do you propose to find those answers?" Danny inquired.

"The obvious place to start," he said, "is Chicago."

"Chicago?" Was he just grasping at straws, or what?

"That's where all this started," he reasoned. "That's where the law firm has its offices."

"That's the law firm representing my benefactor?" It was at least starting to make sense to her now.

Mitch nodded.

"They've already refused to give us any answers," she reminded him. "What makes you think that's going to change any time soon?"

"Because I'm going to Chicago," he told her.

Danny couldn't hide her surprise. "What for?" she asked, puzzled, watching as he unwrapped one of those peppermints he was always eating.

"Answers, obviously."

"You really think going there will make any difference?" she asked dubiously. Why would going there make them reveal what they'd already repeatedly refused to divulge?

He nodded. "Past experience has proven that it does," he answered confidently. "Meeting the parties involved, making contacts within the law firm itself, research—it's all par for the course."

Danny thought about it for a moment. "Maybe you're right," she said finally. It might work, at that.

"I know I am." His tone was confident.

"I'm going with you," she said promptly.

This obviously took him by surprise. "No, you're not," he said, struggling to recover from that surprise.

"You can't stop me," she pointed out. "Last I heard, this was still a free country."

"You'd be in the way," he said in an attempt to dissuade her. She had no idea how much of a distraction she would be.

"I might be able to help. You never know," she told him. He had to know by now that she never took no for an answer.

Didn't he?

"It's not a good idea," Mitch maintained.

"It's not open for discussion."

"This is my job, Danny," he reminded her.

"It's *my* life," she said. "I am going."

Chapter Seven

Their flight into Chicago's O'Hare International Airport arrived half an hour late at nine forty-five in the morning. "I forgot how crazy this place can get," Danny told Mitch as they waited for their luggage to appear on the specified baggage carousel. "It's been at least four years since the last time I was here." She looked around, observing the chaos that surrounded them. "The last time was for a photo shoot for one of the travel magazines."

It's been longer than that for me, Mitch thought, but said nothing. He hadn't been back since the day he moved out of his father's house—not for a visit, not for holidays, not for any reason. Not since his eighteenth birthday. He hadn't seen his father since then, hadn't heard from him.

No one could ever say we were close, he thought dismally. We wouldn't even qualify as passing acquaintances if it weren't for the genetic connection.

He no longer even thought of it as home. How could this be home when the only memories it held for him were unpleasant?

While he looked for a skycap to hail a cab for them, Danny gathered her small suitcase and camera bag and tried to find a ride on her own.

"I don't need somebody to find a cab for me," she told Mitch as the cab pulled up to the curb in front of them. "I usually have better luck on my own, anyway."

Mitch only smiled. That didn't surprise him at all. Not at all. He could see Danny getting a cab with no trouble. He could see Danny stopping traffic anywhere.

He helped her into the back seat, amazed even as he did that she'd permit him to do so. She was so fiercely independent—but then, that was one of the things he loved about her.

Loved?

Was that the word I used? he thought, stunned. Did I say I loved her?

That one had really sneaked up on him.

Do I love Danny?

He started to feel a little panicky. Make that a lot panicky.

Heaven help me if I do!

Now that he thought about it, really thought about it, he had to ask himself if he even knew what love really was. Growing up as he did, he had no first-hand experience with love, no basis for comparison. His mother had died when he was too young to observe his parents' relationship. But then, he wasn't sure it would have shown him anything about a good relationship even if he had been older. His grandfather had said his mother loved his father, but he'd had serious doubts that his father felt anything remotely like love for her. Mitch recalled some of the women his father had brought home over the years. Even as a child, he'd known his father's need for those women had nothing to do with love.

Danny poked him, interrupting his thoughts. "Earth to Mitch!"

He jerked. "Huh?"

She laughed. "You were a million miles away!"

He forced a smile. "No, not nearly that far," he assured her.

"Something I should know about?" she asked.

Mitch shook his head. "No, not yet, anyway," he said quietly. He couldn't just blurt it out like an idiot. No . . . he was going to have to think about this. He had to be sure.

"I should warn you that I hate being kept in suspense," she told him promptly.

He grinned. "Thanks for the warning." He had the distinct feeling that he'd be a whole lot safer if he didn't have feelings for her. This woman was trouble with a capital *T*. Any man who fell for her was doomed.

They checked into the Drake Hotel, the grandest of the city's hotels, which resembled an Italian Renaissance palace, and were escorted to their rooms—adjoining rooms, as it turned out. Danny shot Mitch a suspicious look when she discovered this. "Adjoining rooms?" she asked.

"I didn't request this," Mitch insisted, protesting perhaps a bit too much.

"You made the reservations," she reminded him.

"I didn't request adjoining rooms!"

"Right."

The bellhop intervened then. "You will be perfectly safe, miss," he promised, amused. "The door locks. See?" He handed her the key to that door.

She made a face at Mitch over the bellhop's shoulder. Mitch tried not to laugh.

"I misjudged you, Newman," she said after taking a moment to look around.

"Oh? In what way?" he asked.

"I never would have believed you'd make reservations in a place like this," she told him, referring to the spacious rooms with the dark wood and floral upholstery. "I had you pegged as the roadside-motel type."

He winced. "Thanks a lot."

"You know what I mean."

"Unfortunately, I do."

After the bellhop retreated, tip in hand, Danny and Mitch went to their rooms to unpack and change clothes before tackling the law offices of Fordyce, Baker and Hodge. Alone for the first time since they had left New York, Mitch stood at the window, not really paying any attention to the view. He was thinking—thinking about his father and the relationship they'd never had, about Danny and the relationship that could be.

If he let it.

Did he want to see his father while he was in town? He couldn't think of a single good reason to do so. His father hadn't made any attempts to contact him since he left Chicago, and Mitch was certain Randall Newman had made numerous business trips to New York over the years. The only possible conclusion Mitch could reach, under the circumstances, was that the elder Newman had no interest in seeing his only son.

No more, he thought dismally, than I have in seeing him.

His thoughts turned to Danny. There was plenty of interest where she was concerned, but was he ready to tell her he loved her? He was having a hard time admitting it to himself at this point. That had to mean he was still a long way from any kind of emotional commitment.

Didn't it?

The offices of Fordyce, Baker and Hodge, on the sixteenth floor of an elegant high rise on Lake Shore

Drive, overlooked Lake Michigan. Danny decided it
looked like a law office, from the rich, dark panel-
ing to the volumes of leather-bound books, to the
conservatively dressed, middle-aged receptionist with
the upper-crust British accent.

"I'll bet they advertised for that specific type," she
told Mitch, keeping her voice low so no one else
could hear her. "I can imagine what kind of ad they
ran—receptionist wanted, must look and sound like
she's related to the queen of England, commoners
need not apply."

"Mr. Newman, Ms. Vine?"

They both looked up at the same time. The man
addressing them was of average height and build,
with blue eyes behind horn-rimmed glasses, and an
open, friendly face. "I'm Andrew Baker," he introduced himself. They all shook hands.

"We're supposed to meet with Barbara Fordyce," Mitch told him.

Baker nodded. "Barbara's running a little late,"
he explained. "She'll be joining us shortly."

He took them to a spacious corner office fur-
nished with obviously expensive antiques and an
abundance of green plants. The floor-to-ceiling windows offered an even more spectacular view of Lake
Michigan than they had from their hotel rooms.
They seated themselves around the desk and a secretary served hot tea.

"Newman," Baker said, as if trying to place the name. "You're not related to Randall Newman, are you?"

Mitch frowned. "Distantly," he responded curtly.

Danny studied him for a moment. She got the distinct feeling there was a lot more going on inside him than he was letting on. Who was this Randall Newman, and what was his connection to Mitch? Whatever it was, one thing was certain—it wasn't one he cared to acknowledge.

She looked up as a woman came into the office. She was tall, slender and attractive in a conservative kind of way. Her dark hair was pulled back into a neat bun, and the only jewelry she wore was a Rolex watch and pearl earrings. Her glasses were simple black frames, and she was dressed in a dove gray suit with matching pumps and a white blouse.

She looks like a lawyer, Danny decided. A lawyer who makes a lot of money.

"I'm Barbara Fordyce," she introduced herself, shaking hands with both of them. She moved behind the desk and seated herself. "I have to admit that this visit comes as a surprise," she told them.

"I don't see why," Mitch responded before Danny could. "You had to expect Ms. Vine to be curious."

"Curious, perhaps," Barbara Fordyce conceded with a slight nod, "but most people wouldn't ask too many questions where this kind of money is involved."

Danny spoke up. "I'm not most people, Ms. Fordyce," she said firmly. "I'm not about to accept a bequest, especially one so large, without knowing who left it to me and why."

The attorney was silent for a moment. "You would be a millionaire, Ms. Vine," she pointed out. "Does anything else really matter?"

"Yes, it does," Danny responded with total honesty.

Barbara Fordyce drew in a deep breath. "I'm sorry to hear that," she said quietly. "It was very important to my client that the bulk of his estate go to you."

He, Danny thought. Well, that's something. Not much, but something.

My mysterious benefactor is a he.

"Apparently not too important," Mitch said. "He didn't want her to know who he was."

"Maybe he thought it wouldn't matter," Andrew Baker suggested.

"I don't see why it wouldn't," Mitch argued.

"He had his reasons" was all Barbara Fordyce would say.

"I'm sure. But surely you can understand my client's position," Mitch said carefully. "How can she accept the money without knowing where it came from?"

"What difference does it make, Mr. Newman?"

"It could make a great deal of difference if your client were involved in something illegal," he pointed out.

She laughed aloud at the thought. "I assure you, none of my clients are involved in anything even remotely illegal," she said confidently.

"Then why wouldn't your client allow his identity to be revealed to me?" Danny questioned.

"Personal reasons."

"I'm sure," Mitch said.

Barbara Fordyce shook her head. "I'm sorry," she said quietly. "I had hoped this matter could be resolved to everyone's satisfaction, but apparently it can't."

"Apparently not." Danny rose to her feet. "I'm sorry."

The attorney nodded. "So am I."

"Are you saying you're refusing the money?" Baker asked, concerned.

"Under these conditions, that's exactly what I'm saying," Danny told him.

He looked stunned but made no attempt to discuss it further. It was Mitch who raised the obvious question.

"If Danny doesn't accept it, who does it go to?"

Barbara Fordyce didn't hesitate. "Charity."

"Good," Danny said promptly. "At least it'll be put to good use."

Mitch said nothing more, just got to his feet and nodded politely as he followed Danny out of the office.

"Is this the end of it?" he asked when they reached the elevators.

"The end of what?" Danny asked.

"The inheritance. Are you really turning it down?"

"If she's not going to tell me where it's coming from, yes."

"You really don't care about the money, do you?"

"No," she said as they stepped into an empty elevator. "I don't."

"I think you threw them for a loop back there," he said with a chuckle. "They didn't think there was any way on earth you'd walk away from all that money."

"The only problem is," she began slowly, "if I just turn it down flat, I'll never know who left it to me, or why."

"That's what really matters to you, isn't it?"

She nodded. Somebody cared enough to leave her a fortune. Why didn't that person want her to know who he was?

They had dinner at one of the three restaurants in the hotel. Mitch ordered the closest thing he could find on the menu to a simple meat-and-potatoes entrée—a sirloin steak, medium-rare, with a baked potato with sour cream and chives and a salad he probably wouldn't eat. Danny, adventurous as always, chose the one item on the menu she'd never tried before, an exotic-sounding seafood dish that included shark and swordfish. "I like to try new things," she told him.

"Obviously." He grinned. "Seems a little risky to me, though."

She smiled. "I've left a lot of food on a lot of plates in a lot of places," she admitted. "But you never know how you're going to feel about something unless you give it a try."

How true that is, he thought, but not just about food.

The waiter came promptly, took their order and left them alone again. "I guess you'll want to return to New York right away," he said with a sigh of resignation.

She shook her head. "Not really," she said. "I thought if we stuck around, they might reconsider, or we might unearth something on our own."

"We might at that," he said with a nod, making a few suggestions as to where they might look.

"You seem to know your way around here," Danny observed as they ate.

He shrugged. "Stay in one hotel, you've stayed in them all," he answered evasively.

"I'm not talking about the hotel. I'm talking about Chicago." She took a bite of her food and chewed thoughtfully.

Again he shrugged. "Sometimes my work requires travel."

"So does mine, but I've never gotten to know a city as well as you know this one," she observed.

"I'm a P.I.," he reminded her. "I have to know my way around."

She nodded, seeming to have accepted that explanation. Several minutes passed before she spoke again. "Who's Randall Newman?" she asked.

He didn't answer right away. "Someone from my past," he answered reluctantly.

"A relative?"

"Biologically speaking."

She gave him a quizzical look. "Biologically?"

"Randall Newman is my father."

Danny couldn't hide her surprise. "You say it like it's a dirty word," she noted.

He frowned. "In this case, it is."

She hesitated, apparently not sure if she should pursue the subject further. "Want to talk about it?" she asked after a brief deliberation.

"There's not much to tell."

"I don't mind."

Their conversation was briefly interrupted by their waiter, who brought dinner. After he was gone, Danny turned back to Mitch, still waiting for a response.

Mitch avoided her eyes. "I was an only child. My mother died when I was barely two years old—she was hit by a drunk driver."

"I'm sorry," Danny said softly.

He knew she meant it. "So am I." He paused. "My father was—is—an attorney here. A very successful, very well-known attorney. Single fatherhood wasn't part of his game plan, so I was raised by our housekeeper. She was a terrific lady, but it just wasn't the same as a parent. So, as soon as I was old enough, I hit the road."

"I take it you and your father haven't had much contact since," she concluded.

"We haven't had any contact since," he corrected.

"You haven't even tried?"

"He hasn't tried. It's a two-way street."

She took a bite, thoughtful for a long moment. "How do you feel about your father now?" she asked carefully.

He shrugged. "I don't feel like he's my father, that's for sure," he answered honestly.

"That's understandable."

"I don't really feel much of anything for him, one way or the other," Mitch continued, talking as he cut his steak. "I guess we weren't together enough to have had a relationship at all, good or bad."

"He never spent any time at all with you?"

He shook his head. "Not that I can recall," he said. "I only saw him coming and going—going off to the office, coming home long enough to change or make phone calls before heading out for a business meeting or dinner. I might see him late at night if I was still awake when he finally came home.'' He didn't mention that he'd cried himself to sleep most of those nights, feeling unloved and unwanted, certain his father saw him only as a burden, an inconvenience to be tolerated.

''My father was an attorney, too—and later a judge—but he was always there for his family,'' Danny remembered. ''As far as I can recall, he didn't miss many evenings or weekends with his kids.''

''I used to think my father looked for excuses to avoid spending time with me,'' Mitch confided. It did seem that way—no matter when he asked for his father or what the problem was, Randall never had time for him.

His clients mattered more to him than I did.

''I can't imagine having such a rotten childhood,'' she said, clearly at a loss for words.

He was silent for a while. ''Is that why you refused to believe your parents could have any knowledge of this business?'' he asked, not at all sure how she'd respond.

''No, I didn't believe it because I know my parents well enough to know they wouldn't have kept anything so important from me,'' she told him.

''Maybe if they thought they were protecting you—'' he started.

''Not even then,'' she said, shaking her head emphatically. ''My parents were always totally honest with us about everything.''

''Even when it hurt?''

"Especially then!"

Mitch thought she was being too defensive but didn't push it. He was still convinced the Vines were hiding something, but he had no proof.

Not yet, anyway.

Danny Vine turned out to be the first woman he'd taken to dinner who even *ordered* dessert, let alone ate it. She consumed the rich chocolate treat with genuine gusto. Mitch was amused and fascinated at the same time—she was the kind of woman he'd always hoped to find. A woman who wasn't afraid of anything, including enjoying her dinner.

Do I tell her now or not? he asked himself again.

The decision was made for him less than an hour later, when they left the restaurant and went upstairs to their rooms. Outside Danny's door, they paused to say good-night.

"I'll give you this," Danny said lightly, "you sure know how to show a girl a good time."

He grinned. "You consider *this* a good time?" he asked.

"Sure. You bring me here to Chicago, we stay at one of the best hotels, eat in the best restaurants, *and* try to unravel a mystery," she said.

"You make it sound so romantic," he observed, amused.

"In a way it is, don't you think?" She gave him a smile and a wink that dissolved what little was left of his self-control.

He was tempted to tell her what he thought. He was tempted to tell her how he felt about her. He was tempted to show her how he felt.

Then it happened.

Looking into her eyes, feeling her so close, he found himself wanting to be even closer...moving closer...touching her hair...then their lips met, hesitantly at first, then with an urgency matched by her ardent response.

He slipped an arm around her waist, drawing her to him. She put her arms around his neck, clinging to him as if she were afraid he might let go.

Chapter Eight

Did it really happen?

Danny still wasn't sure when she woke the next morning, alone in bed in her own room, that it wasn't just a dream. She remembered being outside her door with Mitch—she'd been getting strange vibes from him all evening—and all at once they were kissing. That was some kiss, she remembered now, sitting up in bed, willing the fog of an unusually heavy sleep to lift from her brain. She ran her fingers through her hair, pushing it away from her face. Some kiss, indeed. A long way from a friendly little peck on the cheek. Harness the energy in that kiss and you could light up Times Square for a year. Really packed a wallop. I'm surprised we were able to stop there.

Assuming we *did* stop there.

Surely we did.

She had to assume they had, since she was definitely alone in bed. That, and the absence of any memory of anything beyond the kiss. If anything like that had happened between them, she'd definitely remember it.

It wasn't the kind of thing one was likely to forget. She certainly wouldn't have forgotten it, not even for a moment, no matter how soundly she'd slept. Not after waiting so long, so anxiously for something to happen between them.

She thought about it. They had kissed—tenderly at first, then eagerly, then with an overpowering hunger that demanded to be consummated.

But it wasn't

No, it wasn't. It definitely wasn't. He'd been the one who withdrew. He had stopped before either of them lost control.

Before he lost control, she mentally corrected herself. I was already well past the point of no return.

Then it hit her.

I'm falling in love with him!

But he'd held back. He'd been the one to withdraw. He was the one who stopped them from going too far—whatever "too far" was in their case.

Hearing a knock at the door, she slipped into her black-and-white kimono-style robe and went to answer it. She thought it would be Mitch, ready to go downstairs for breakfast—had she overslept, or what?—until she opened the door and saw the bell-hop.

"Room service," he announced, grinning broadly.

This was weird. "I didn't order room service," she told him. Unless I've forgotten that, too.

Must've been some night.

"This might explain." The bellhop handed her a small envelope.

She opened it. It was a note from Mitch:

Danny—
Sorry I couldn't have breakfast with you but something came up. I'll explain everything when I get back.

                                           Mitch

She looked up at the bellhop, forcing a smile she didn't really feel. "Put it over there," she said, indicating where she wanted him to park the cart.

He nodded. "Yes, ma'am."

She waited for him to give her the bill, but there wasn't one. "It's already been taken care of," he told her, waving her off when she tried to get him to give it to her.

"Tip, too?"

He smiled. "Everything."

After he'd gone, she uncovered the plates. Eggs Benedict . . . melon balls . . . fresh orange juice...toasted raisin bread. Mitch had pretty much thought of everything, Danny decided. Everything but providing her with a little breakfast-table companionship.

"Where are you, Mitch?" she wondered aloud. "Avoiding me?"

She decided to find out.

She went to the phone and dialed Mitch's room. It rang several times and was finally transferred to the hotel switchboard.

"Operator."

Danny was puzzled. Maybe she'd dialed the wrong number. "I, uh, I was trying to reach Mitchell Newman's room," she stammered.

"I'm sorry, he's not in his room. Would you like to leave a message?" the operator asked helpfully.

"He's out?"

"Yes, ma'am."

"Do you know what time he left?"

"No, ma'am, I don't. Would you like to leave a message?"

"No. No message."

She hung up. He was avoiding her. He'd ordered breakfast for her, then left the hotel—early, she guessed.

Must be one heck of a guilt trip.

But why? she wondered now. Once the fog of sleep had lifted from her brain, she remembered clearly the events of the night before. They hadn't gone any further than that megawatt kiss at her door, so what did he have to feel guilty about?

Unless . . .

Maybe he had regrets about the kiss. Maybe he wished it hadn't happened. Maybe he was avoiding her now because he was afraid she'd read too much into it and now wanted more from him than he was willing to give. Maybe he was trying to discourage her, let her down as gently as possible. He thought she had expectations, that she wanted some sort of commitment from him. Wasn't that what most men thought most women wanted after the slightest encouragement?

Absurd, she thought as she sat down to her delicious but solitary meal. Do they really think we're all so desperate?

Surely he knows me better than that, she thought as she ate. He knows I'm not the type to pursue a man who's made it clear he's not interested. He knows I'm not desperate. At least not where men are concerned.

And then she remembered the kiss.

The more she thought about it, the more convinced she was that she wasn't reading too much into it, after all. She knew passion when she saw it—and felt it—and there was no mistaking the passion in Mitch's kiss. Or in the way he'd held her. He hadn't wanted to stop there, any more than she'd wanted to stop.

But they had.

That had been his idea, not hers. She hadn't wanted to stop because she was in love with him. But what was he feeling? He had managed to maintain his self-control. Did that mean that his passion wasn't as strong as hers, his feelings weren't as strong as hers?

This is nuts, she told herself.

Danny had never been in love before. Oh, there had been men in her life—men she'd liked, men she'd cared for, men she'd been physically attracted to. But no one she'd loved. This was a new experience for her.

She had a strong feeling it was a new experience for Mitch, too. He seemed somewhat embarrassed that he'd allowed his emotions free reign, even for that few minutes. I suppose I shouldn't be surprised, she thought, remembering what he'd told her about his father and his childhood.

He's reluctant to let himself love anyone, she concluded.

I'm going to have to show him he doesn't have to hold back with me.

"I got your message," Mitch said. "What's this all about?"

The call had come late last night. Barbara Fordyce's secretary explained that her boss had tried to reach Danny, but there had been no answer in her room—she had been there but was probably in the shower, Mitch decided—so she'd had her secretary call him. The executor of the estate wanted to meet Danny, which surprised Mitch.

"Where is she?" the attorney asked now.

"I didn't mention this to her," Mitch answered honestly.

"Why not?"

"Ms. Fordyce, just as you're being paid to look out for your client's interests, I'm paid to look out for my client's," he pointed out. "This hasn't been easy for her. I won't have her subjected to more stress than is absolutely necessary."

"I see."

"Now, what's this all about?" he asked again.

Barbara Fordyce led him back to her office. "After you and Ms. Vine left here yesterday, I had to inform the executors of the estate that Ms. Vine was refusing her inheritance," she explained. "I was, as a result, asked to arrange this meeting."

As he entered the office, a man seated near the desk stood up. He appeared to be in his late sixties—tall, thin, with thick white hair and mustache, wearing what had to be a very expensive suit, gold watch, and gold cuff links. "Mitchell Newman, Franklin Ewing," Barbara Fordyce introduced them. The two men shook hands, then sat down, the older man regarding Mitch with a degree of curiosity.

"Is something wrong?" Mitch asked.

"Newman," Ewing repeated, recognizing the name. "Are you related to Randall Newman?"

Not again. "Distantly," he replied, managing a weak smile. He didn't want to talk about his father, but he decided this didn't really come as a surprise. Not here, of all places. Randall Newman was a big man in Chicago.

"Mr. Ewing is one of the executors of the estate, Mr. Newman," Barbara Fordyce explained, seating herself. "When I told him Ms. Vine refused her inheritance unless she could know who left it to her, he asked to meet with her."

Mitch turned to the older man, unable to hide his surprise. "Is that so?" he asked carefully.

"Where is she?" Ewing asked, obviously quite anxious to meet Danny. It made Mitch somewhat uneasy.

"Back at the hotel," Mitch told him. "I thought I should find out what this is all about before I tell her. She's been through enough with this—"

"Are you an attorney, Mr. Newman?" Ewing asked. His tone had changed to impatience.

Mitch shook his head. "I'm a private investigator," he responded. "Danny—Ms. Vine—hired me to find out who was behind this."

Ewing nodded. "I can understand her concern," he said. "I pleaded with Connor to tell her while he was still alive, but he wouldn't hear of it."

"Connor?" Mitch asked.

"Connor Capshaw, my business partner," he explained. "And my friend for many, many years. Connor and I were friends since boyhood."

Connor Capshaw, Mitch recalled, was one of the ten richest men in the United States. Capshaw & Ewing was one of the most illustrious corporations in the country. "The money was left to Danny by Connor Capshaw?" Mitch asked. This was making less and less sense.

Ewing nodded. "That, and a great deal more," he said.

Mitch gave him a quizzical look. More? More than a million dollars? This was getting stranger by the minute. What was Danny's connection to Connor Capshaw? "Why?" he asked.

"Ms. Vine is Connor's only living heir, Mr. Newman—his granddaughter," Ewing said.

"What?" Mitch couldn't hide his surprise. He'd had his suspicions about Danny's parents, about whether or not they were *really* her parents, almost from the beginning. But he'd never suspected anything like this. He stood up abruptly. "How?"

"Sit down," Ewing suggested, gesturing toward the chair, "and I'll explain."

Mitch nodded, sinking back down slowly into his chair. "I think you'd better," he said. He was thinking of Danny. How could he tell her this? How would she take it?

Franklin Ewing and Barbara Fordyce exchanged glances. "Some years ago—I've lost track of exactly how many—Connor's only son, David, fell in love with a young woman he met in college named Jennifer Scott—a stunning girl, really."

"And his father was against the relationship," Mitch guessed.

"No, he wasn't," Ewing insisted. "David thought he was because he warned David repeatedly not to rush into anything."

"Like marriage?" This was starting to sound very, very predictable. He guessed Jennifer Scott's family was probably several rungs below the Capshaws on

the socioeconomic ladder, therefore unsuitable for
the Capshaw heir—in his father's opinion, anyway.

"Like marriage," Ewing conceded with a nod.
"Connor liked Jennifer, but he felt they were both
too young to get married."

"They were in college?" Mitch asked. Predictable.

"In college, yes, and Connor felt that education
was important, especially since David would one day
inherit an enormous responsibility," Ewing recalled.

"What made him think his son wouldn't stay in
school if he and Jennifer married?" Mitch asked. He
knew Danny would ask these questions, and he
wanted to have answers for her.

"David had told him as much," Ewing answered.
"He said he wasn't interested in what he called 'the
family business,' that he and Jennifer wanted to
travel while they decided what they wanted to do with
their lives."

"I take it that didn't sit well with the senior Capshaw," Mitch said.

Ewing shook his head. "Connor tried to reason
with David, but they had a violent argument," he
said. "That night, David and Jennifer left Chicago."

"Eloped?"

"That was their plan, yes, but it never got that
far."

Mitch gave him a puzzled look.

"There was an accident. No one knows exactly what happened, whether it was the rain or if David had been driving too many hours without sleep, or if they were run off the road. All we knew for many years was that there was an accident in western Pennsylvania. David was killed instantly," Ewing recalled. "Connor got there as quickly as he could, but it was too late."

"What about Jennifer?" Mitch asked. What about Danny? he wondered. Danny was a strong woman. Resilient. Still, he knew this was getting to her. How many times had she come close to refusing the inheritance and forgetting the whole thing? He recalled her response when he suggested her parents might not have been totally honest with her. She'd been upset—angry, actually.

And he thought about last night. The last thing he'd wanted to do was stop kissing her. He had only because he cared so much for her. He loved her. Whatever happened between them would happen only if and when it was right for both of them, not because he took advantage of her vulnerability.

"We never saw her again," Ewing said. "Connor went to the hospital when he found out where she'd been taken, but she was gone. She'd checked herself out."

"Where did she go?"

"No one knew."

"Then how—" Mitch began.

"Jennifer seemed to have vanished from the face of the earth," Ewing continued. "Even her own family hadn't seen or heard from her. Then, a little over two years ago, Connor received a letter from her."

"She's still alive?"

"She was. She died shortly after she wrote Connor," he said. "Ovarian cancer, I believe."

"Why did she write after all those years?" Mitch asked, certain he'd already guessed the answer.

"She knew she was dying and wanted to do so with a clear conscience," Ewing said. "She told Connor she and David had been in a hurry to get married because she was pregnant. They were headed for New York at the time of the accident. When she was told David was dead, something inside her snapped, psychologically speaking. She just left the hospital without her doctor's permission. She went to New York, but apparently didn't fare well there. She told Connor she was barely able to make ends meet."

"So she didn't keep the baby," Mitch concluded. He remembered his investigation in New York—the absence of Danny's birth certificate or other documentation. How had the Vines done it? he wondered now. How had they managed to keep Danny from finding out? Surely she'd needed a birth certificate to get her driver's license, to go to college.

Well, her father *is* a judge, he reminded himself.

Ewing shook his head. "No. She said she wanted to, but in the end did what she felt was best for the child."

"Why didn't she just go to Mr. Capshaw then?" Mitch asked.

"She and David believed Connor would do anything to keep them apart," Ewing reminded him. "She didn't believe he would be willing to help her and her baby."

"Was she wrong?"

"Most definitely," Ewing answered without hesitation. "He would have done anything for that child—and for Jennifer—had he known."

"Did Jennifer know who adopted her baby?" Mitch asked.

"No, and that was killing her," the older man told him. "Jennifer never married. Her devotion to David was much stronger than any of us could have guessed. Years later, she tried—unsuccessfully—to find her child, but she was unable to find out who'd adopted the baby. All she did know was that she had given birth to a baby girl."

"She couldn't find out, but Connor Capshaw could?"

"Arrogant as this is going to sound, Mr. Newman, money talks," Ewing reminded him. "Connor spent two years and a great deal of money looking for his granddaughter."

"And finally found her."

Franklin Ewing nodded. "He found out who she was, where she lived, what she did for a living," he said. "He learned everything he could about his granddaughter."

"Why didn't he ever try to see her?" Mitch asked.

"He did," Ewing revealed. "He met her—several times, in fact."

"Oh?"

"He went to her studio a number of times," Ewing revealed. "He tried to get to know her without making her suspicious."

"Apparently he succeeded." Mitch couldn't recall Danny ever mentioning having met Connor Capshaw.

"Capshaw & Ewing does a great deal of advertising," Ewing went on. "Connor made sure she got all of the photographic work."

"I'm sure she appreciated that," Mitch said.

"He would have done anything for her," Ewing said. "He would have gone to any lengths to be near her."

Next question, Mitch thought.

"Why didn't he ever tell her who he was—the truth, I mean?"

"Before he saw her for the first time, he went to see the Vines," Ewing explained. "They told him they'd never told her she was adopted. They pleaded with him not to tell her."

"And?"

"In the end, he did what he felt was best for her."

"Didn't he think this inheritance would raise a lot of questions?" Mitch asked.

"He hoped she wouldn't ask too many questions."

"If he got to know her at all, he had to know she would," Mitch pointed out.

"What are you saying?" Ewing asked carefully.

"That maybe he did this hoping she would find out without him telling her," Mitch reasoned.

"Absurd."

"Is it?"

"If he'd wanted to tell her, he would have," Ewing maintained. "He would have made sure she knew about the entire inheritance."

"Entire inheritance?"

"The bequest she was told about is only part of it," Ewing told him. "A small part."

Mitch studied him for a moment. "Maybe you'd better explain."

"Danielle Vine is Connor Capshaw's sole heir," Ewing explained. "As his sole heir, she inherits all that was his—his home in Lake Forest, all of his money and personal assets, all of his stock in Capshaw & Ewing."

"You're kidding!"

"This is no joke, I assure you," Ewing responded. "What will you tell her now?" he asked after a tense pause.

"The truth."

"All of it?"

Mitch nodded. "All of it. That, after all, is what I was hired to do," he said, getting to his feet. "Uncover the truth."

"If she wants to see me, I'll be happy to—"

"I'll tell her," Mitch assured him.

But as he left the office, he found himself wondering what he *was* going to tell her.

And how she was going to react.

Chapter Nine

"I thought maybe you'd ducked out on me," Danny told Mitch when he returned to the hotel.

"Ducked out?" He looked genuinely confused.

Or was it confusion? On second look, she decided he looked more nervous than confused. Like maybe he was hiding something—or avoiding something.

Or someone.

"After last night—"

"I'm not sorry about last night," he told her. "There was so much I wanted to say to you..." His voice trailed off.

"Was?" she asked. Had he changed his mind, or what? This man made less sense than anyone she had ever known.

"Unfortunately, it's going to have to wait—for now," he said tightly. His eyes met hers for the first time since he'd come through the door. "I've been at Barbara Fordyce's office."

"They've reconsidered?" That was hard to believe.

He nodded.

"Why didn't you tell me?" she asked. "I should have been there."

She felt a faint sense of unease. He knew something.

Something she'd come here to find out. But now she wasn't at all sure she wanted to know.

"You were apparently in the shower when they called," he said, taking off his coat, "so they asked for me. I figured you'd already been through enough, so I decided to see what they wanted before telling you about it."

He was trying to protect her. He did care—apparently more than he was willing to admit. So why was he holding back?

Frustrating, she thought.

"And?"

"Do you remember meeting a man named Connor Capshaw?" he asked.

She nodded. "Everyone knows who Connor Capshaw is, Mitch," she reminded him. Connor Capshaw was one of the richest men in the country, and his conglomerate, Capshaw & Ewing, owned department stores and pharmaceutical companies and airlines and more—much, much more. She'd met him a few times—more than a few, actually—when she was hired to do the photography for Capshaw & Ewing's advertising and public relations. She remembered thinking it odd that he'd met with her personally, but decided he was either eccentric or some kind of control freak.

"Was," he corrected.

"That's right, he died recently—wait a minute!" She stared at him in disbelief. "Oh, no, you're not going to try to tell me that Connor Capshaw left me a million dollars."

"That, and a great deal more." He was serious. This couldn't be—no—but he *was* serious!

"That's absurd," she insisted. "Why would Connor Capshaw leave anything to me?"

It didn't make any sense. But now that she thought about it, nothing about Connor Capshaw had made sense.

Did he have some kind of weird crush on her, or what? He sure hadn't seemed like the type.

He frowned. "Because you're his granddaughter," he said quietly.

"His granddaughter?" She felt her heart leap into her throat.

"That's what they claim."

Danny shook her head emphatically. "They're wrong," she stated flatly.

"Are they?"

"It's not possible!" she cried.

"Isn't it?"

One look at his face told her what he was thinking. "No, it's not!" she snapped. How could he even suggest such a thing.

"Danny—" he started.

Now she was angry. "Are you going to start that again?" she demanded hotly.

"It's true, Danny," he said, drawing in a deep breath.

"It can't be!" Tears came to her eyes, try as she did to hold them back. "It's not possible!"

This is a nightmare, she thought desperately. This can't be happening. No, Mom and Dad would have told me. They wouldn't have kept anything like this from me!

The thought brought a fresh flow of tears to her eyes. She'd always thought she could handle anything, but not this.

"Are you so sure about that?" he asked carefully.

"My parents would have told me!" she cried. "They would never have kept anything like this from me!"

He seemed so cold, so remote now. Trying to make her heart accept something she couldn't.

Wouldn't accept.

He tried to reach out to her, but she pushed him away. "It's not true!" she insisted. "It can't be true! They're lying! They have to be lying!"

"Why would they lie about it?" he questioned.

"I don't know. Maybe they've confused me with somebody else," she sobbed. "Anyway, if I'm this man's granddaughter, why was I put up for adoption?"

"Because your mother—"

She cut him off. "Millie Vine is my mother!" she snapped. That was the reality, *her* reality. Even if it were true—not that she believed for a minute that it was—the people she knew as her parents would always be her parents no matter what.

"All right!" He raised a hand to silence her. "Your *biological* mother was a young woman, a college student named Jennifer Scott who fell in love with Connor Capshaw's only son, David. They wanted to get married."

"But Papa Capshaw was against it, right?" Danny concluded.

It wasn't uncommon. Rich boy falls hard for beautiful girl from wrong side of the tracks, she thought. *Romeo and Juliet* revisited.

But it had nothing to do with her.

Or did it?

She wished she hadn't come here.

"Not exactly," he said. "He just wanted David to finish his education first."

"I'll bet." He was probably just stalling for time, looking for a way to split them up. He probably thought Jennifer wasn't good enough for the Capshaw heir.

"There was a misunderstanding of sorts," Mitch continued. "David and Jennifer eloped—or tried to."

"Tried to? Let me guess. Daddy headed them off at the pass."

"They were driving, headed for New York. There was an accident, and David was killed," he told her.

"And Jennifer?" Now she wasn't sure what to expect. Had Jennifer been killed in the accident? Died in childbirth? What?

Why didn't I stay in New York?

"She disappeared from the hospital. Until a few years ago, no one knew where she was," Mitch said.

"A few years ago?"

"She was dying—cancer, they said—and she wrote to Capshaw," he explained. "Before she died, she wanted him to know he had a granddaughter."

Danny frowned. "Nice of her," she muttered.

If this Jennifer had really been her mother—her biological mother—why hadn't she kept her? Why hadn't Connor Capshaw taken his granddaughter? If Jennifer hadn't been able or willing to raise a child alone, surely she could have made David's father aware of her pregnancy. She could have offered him the opportunity to raise his only grandchild.

Jennifer didn't tell him, she reminded herself.

Until it was too late.

"She was scared, Danny," he said softly. "She was young, pregnant and alone in New York. She didn't think she could go home, and she was convinced Connor Capshaw had been opposed to her relationship with David. She apparently wasn't sure what he might or might not do, and I guess it was a chance she just wasn't willing to take. She was probably afraid to tell him. She felt she had to do what was best for her baby."

"Adoption."

If, by some chance, Jennifer Scott really was her mother, she had at least done what was best for her baby, as she claimed to have wanted to do.

I couldn't have had a better life than the one I've had, she thought now.

Not even if I'd grown up in the Capshaw's lap of luxury.

He nodded. "In her letter to Capshaw, she said she'd wanted to keep the baby—you—but didn't feel she could provide for you," he recalled. "Years later, she tried to find you but failed."

"Apparently my grandfather didn't have that problem," Danny said coldly.

Why couldn't he have left it alone? He obviously wasn't concerned with what was best for her. Or maybe he was. People like Connor Capshaw never believed anyone could do anything as well as they could.

"He had the money and the connections to get things done."

"Obviously."

She wondered how many people he'd paid off to gain access to sealed adoption records. How much had it cost him?

Maybe he did care, she conceded. But did it really matter now?

"When he found out about you," Mitch went on, "he used that money and those connections to find you. He went to see your parents first. When they told him they'd never told you that you were adopted, he agreed not to do so, but insisted on seeing you."

Danny thought about it. "He came to the studio a number of times," she recalled. She remembered him as being a kindly old man who dressed like a million dollars. He'd been friendly, with an uncommon interest in her and everything she was doing. Phoebe had kidded her about holding out for marriage. Phoebe thought the old guy had a crush on Danny. She continued, "He didn't act like the VIP he was—just a very nice old man who seemed fascinated by me and my work, for whatever reason." She paused. "For whatever reason!" That was a laugh! Phoebe had never been so far off base!

"He obviously cared," Mitch said then. "He went to a lot of trouble to find you."

"Yeah." She paced the floor nervously. "I'm still not convinced they've got the right person."

He was silent for a moment. "Franklin Ewing— that's the guy I talked to—said he'd be happy to talk to you, answer any questions you might have."

She nodded slowly. "That might be a good idea. Yes, I'd like to talk to him."

"Danny, this is Franklin Ewing," Mitch introduced the older man. "He's the executor of Connor Capshaw's estate."

She studied him for a long moment. He was about the same age as Connor Capshaw—or the same age

Connor Capshaw had been the last time she'd seen him. He had the same elegant look, wore the same kind of expensive suit and jewelry. The same surprising warmth.

I must have a tattoo on my forehead reading "heiress," Danny decided.

Ewing took her hand. "I was also his close friend," he said, smiling. "I am so pleased to finally meet his only granddaughter."

Danny didn't smile. "You seem awfully sure you've got the right woman," she commented. She now considered it a possibility but still had serious doubts.

"We are absolutely certain," he assured her.

"How can you be?" she questioned. She wasn't about to simply take their word for it. She had to have proof.

She turned to Mitch, wanting desperately to reach out to him, wanting him to hold her, wanting him to make everything all right, but knowing it wasn't possible.

Nothing was ever going to be all right again.

"Our people are nothing if not thorough," he said simply.

"Our people?" Danny gave a weak laugh. "You sound like the CIA." Probably not too far from the truth, Danny decided. She wouldn't be at all surprised to find he had connections there, as well.

Or even higher up, for that matter.

"No, we're not the CIA," he said, slightly amused, "but we are quite thorough."

"I'm sure." There wasn't too much she *was* sure of at this point, but she was sure of that.

She looked at Mitch again. He gave her an encouraging smile. She wished he'd give her more.

"I'm sure you must have many questions," he said then. "Ask me anything you like."

"All right," she said with a nod, "tell me why."

They all seated themselves. Mitch sat next to Danny, moving his chair closer. He reached out and took her hand, giving it a reassuring squeeze.

Danny looked at him, managing a slight smile. She did love him. If only they could just forget about all of this and take the next flight back to New York. If only none of this had ever happened.

But then, if none of this had happened, she and Mitch probably would never have met.

She thought about it. Maybe all things did happen for a reason, after all.

"Why?"

"Yes. Why, after all these years he had to find me, intrude on my life?" she started. "Why did he have to leave his fortune to me? Why did he try to prevent David and Jennifer from getting married? For starters."

"Your grandfather wasn't opposed to a marriage between David and Jennifer—he was only concerned that they were rushing into it."

"For obvious reasons," Danny pointed out. She knew she was being too defensive, but couldn't help herself.

"Connor didn't know Jennifer was pregnant," Ewing told her.

"Would it have made any difference?" Danny asked.

She wasn't quite sure why knowing that mattered so much to her, but it did. If Connor Capshaw really was her grandfather, she needed to know he would have accepted her then, that he hadn't just tracked her down out of a sense of guilt in his later years, when he knew his time was running out.

"Of course it would have! Connor was devastated when he learned he had a granddaughter and that she—you—had been placed for adoption."

"But he couldn't leave well enough alone, could he?"

"You were his only living relative," Ewing reminded her. "In his place, could you just walk away?"

Danny hesitated. "I don't know what I'd do," she finally admitted. That much was true. She really wasn't sure what she'd do.

"Connor was desperate to find you. There was nothing he would not have done to find out what had become of you."

"What about my—Jennifer?" Danny asked. Hadn't he said Jennifer was ill? Hadn't he said she had cancer, that she was dying?

Danny felt the stirring of an emotion she couldn't understand or even identify. Could it be grief for the mother she never knew?

Ewing frowned. "Jennifer, I'm sorry to say, passed away shortly before we located you," he said.

"I'd like to see photos of them," Danny said promptly. That would help. That would most definitely help.

"I anticipated that you might," he said, reaching for a large leather binder on the desk. "This is the Capshaw family album, 1939 to 1969."

Danny took it, looking at him questioningly. "They're all in here?" She wanted to look, needed to look, yet a part of her was afraid to.

"All of them," he answered with a patient smile.

Taking a deep breath, she put it on her lap and opened it, turning the pages slowly. There were photos of Connor Capshaw and his late wife, Eugenie...photos of David as a baby, as a toddler, as a boy...David's graduation from high school—no doubt some expensive private school. And, toward the end of the album, photos of David and Jennifer.

Looking at those photos, Danny could no longer deny her genetic heritage. She had her father's eyes and nose, her mother's mouth and chin. And Jennifer's hair—thick and red and curly, exactly like her own.

She looked at Mitch. He was concerned. It was written all over his face. That, and more. Danny's heart was breaking when she turned back to the photo album.

It's true, she thought. I am their child.

* * *

"Talk to me, Danny," Mitch urged.

They were, at Danny's insistence, on a flight bound for New York. She hadn't said much of anything since they left the offices of Fordyce, Baker and Hodge, other than to tell him she needed to return to New York *now*. She had to see her parents— the Vines—*now*, she said. She had to know why they'd kept the truth from her.

She was hurting. He had only to look at her to know it. The normally open, smiling face was contorted with pain, the shining eyes red from crying.

She looked at him, frowning. "I don't know what to say," she confessed. "I don't know what to think, what to feel."

"That's understandable," he told her. "This has been a shock." He did the only thing he could think of to do. He put an arm around her, drawing her close. She snuggled against him, crying softly.

"The understatement of the year," she said, dabbing the corners of her eyes with a tissue that was past ready for the waste can.

He wished he knew what to do for her. He wanted desperately to reach out to her, to tell her everything was going to be all right. The problem was that he didn't know what to do, what to tell her. When it came to anything of an emotional nature, he was at a loss. He could tell her he loved her, but would that comfort her now, or would it just confuse her more?

He decided to wait.

"What are you going to do?" he asked. "When we get back to New York, I mean."

Danny shook her head. "I'm not sure," she confessed. "I do know I have to see them, talk to them."

"Your parents?"

She nodded. "I have to know why they didn't tell me."

"Then you *are* going to Troy?"

That worried him. No matter what her parents said to her right now, it might be more then she could handle. He wished she'd wait but knew it would do no good to suggest she do so.

"I have to. I can't do this over the phone."

"After you've had a good night's sleep—"

Danny shook her head. "It can't wait," she insisted. "I have to go tonight, as soon as we land."

"You shouldn't be driving," he told her. "You're exhausted, certainly too tired to drive."

"*I have to,*" she stressed.

"Then I'll go with you," he said promptly. He could drive. That would be best. He could be with her, help her deal with whatever she found waiting for her in Troy. He could love her—

"No—I mean, I love you for wanting to go through this with me," she started. "But no, I have to do this alone."

He opened his mouth to argue but thought better of the idea. It wouldn't do any good. Danny could be so infuriatingly stubborn sometimes. If she was determined to do this now, she would do it now. If she was set on going alone, she'd go alone. Nothing he could say or do would change her mind.

This is the woman I fell in love with, he thought miserably. This is what I've got to look forward to.

If we even have a future together.

Chapter Ten

Danny sat in her car outside her parents' home for the better part of an hour, trying to summon up the courage to go inside, to confront them and ask the question she wasn't sure she wanted to have answered.

A light went on in their upstairs bedroom. They're up, she thought. Any minute now, Mom will come downstairs to start breakfast. As she had every morning for the past two decades.

She waited until she saw her father come to the door for his morning paper—another age-old ritual in the Vine household—before getting out of her car. He looked up when she slammed the car door. "Danny!" he said, smiling. "Not often you're around for breakfast anymore."

She gave him a halfhearted hug and followed him into the house, where her mother had heard her voice and came to see what was going on. "I have to talk to the two of you," Danny told them.

Millie and Harris exchanged perplexed looks.

"Do you know a man named Connor Capshaw?" Danny wanted to know.

The Vines exchanged unmistakably nervous glances before her father made a hasty but futile attempt to cover up. "I don't know too many people who don't know who Connor Capshaw is, dear," he pointed out. "His name is all over our bathroom—and probably most of our neighbors', as well."

Danny's patience wore thinner by the minute. "That's not what I mean," she started carefully, "and I think you know it."

So much for hoping this was a mistake, she thought. It couldn't be any more obvious than it was at this moment that they'd been hiding the truth for a very long time.

Millie bit her lower lip. "You know, don't you?" she asked in a voice filled with dread.

The older woman was fighting back tears. Tears of guilt? Danny wondered. Under any other circumstances, Danny would have rushed to comfort her mother, but this time she was too consumed by her own pain to do anything.

Danny frowned. "That I'm adopted? That Connor Capshaw is my biological grandfather?" She nodded. "I know. I know most of it." She wished she didn't know. She wished none of this had ever happened, that Connor Capshaw had left his estate to someone else.

She wished for so many things that could never be now.

"Most of it?" Her father gave her a quizzical look, not sure he understood.

"What I don't know—" her voice was trembling now, as was her body "—is why I didn't hear any of this from either of you."

Would it have made any difference? she wondered now. She wasn't sure. She doubted anything either of them could have said or done would have softened the blow.

"We always intended to tell you," her father maintained. "We planned to tell you as soon as you were old enough to understand—"

Danny cut him off. "Why didn't you?" she asked irritably.

She told herself she would have been better able to deal with this if she'd been told as a child that she was adopted. But if she were to be completely honest with herself, she wasn't absolutely certain of that, either.

He seemed at a loss. "Something always happened, the time wasn't right," he said with a lame shrug.

Danny could tell by the look on his face that he knew it was a lame excuse but was unable to come up with anything better.

"The first time, you came home from camp with the worst case of poison ivy I've ever seen. You looked so pitiful, we couldn't bring ourselves to do it."

"By the time we summoned up the courage again," her mother said, "you fell out of that tree in the backyard and broke your arm."

"It's a good thing I was so accident-prone," Danny observed sullenly. She wondered what excuse they would have come up with if she hadn't been the victim of so many childhood mishaps.

"We felt you had a right to know, dear," her father told her, "that we had to tell you."

"But?"

"But there were concerns."

"Concerns?"

"You were the only one of our children who was adopted," her mother explained. "We worried that knowing that would make you feel like an outsider, that it might make you insecure."

That much, at least, made sense to Danny. She'd been a deeply sensitive child beneath that boisterous exterior. Knowing she was the only one of the Vine children who was adopted would definitely have bothered her.

"How do you think I feel now?" she asked, fighting back tears, pushing that thought aside. "I was totally blindsided by this! I wasn't prepared for it. I didn't believe it. I was so sure my parents would never lie to me, I ended up feeling like such a fool!"

That, as long as she was being honest with herself, was what bothered her the most at the moment. She'd trusted them. She'd been so certain they would never lie to her, would never have kept anything so important from her.

She'd been wrong, and that hurt more than anything else.

"We know we were wrong, Danny," her father said quietly. "We should have told you—"

She turned on him angrily. "Yes, you should have!" she snapped. "You should have told me a long time ago. At the very least, you should have told me after Connor Capshaw came to see you!"

Her father couldn't hide his surprise. "You know about that?"

"Of course I know!"

"He said he'd never tell you—" her mother began.

"He didn't. He's dead, remember?"

"But—"

"I met his attorney. I met his closest friend and business partner," Danny said. "They told me. Actually, they told me a lot of things." She was thinking of the photographs, of the things Franklin Ewing and Barbara Fordyce had told her about the Capshaws, about David and Jennifer.

"About Mr. Capshaw's son?"

"Among other things."

Neither of her parents said anything, waiting for her to go on.

"Did you know about the money, the inheritance?" she asked. Connor Capshaw had come to see them. Surely he'd told them. If they knew about the inheritance, they had to know she'd want to have known where it came from!

They both nodded, albeit reluctantly.

"Didn't you think that alone would raise questions?" she asked. "Didn't you think I'd look for answers?"

They both avoided her eyes. "We hoped you wouldn't," her mother said finally.

Her eyes narrowed suspiciously. "You know me better than that," she said coldly. Then, after a long pause, she asked, "How did all of this come about, anyway?"

"Come about?" her father repeated, not quite understanding.

"My adoption," she prompted. "Why did it happen at all? Why adopt a baby when you already had eight kids of your own?"

That was the part that didn't make sense to Danny. Not only had she not known she was adopted, none of her brothers or sisters seemed to know it, either.

"I was pregnant," Millie began haltingly. "We already knew this was going to be our last child. I'd had some medical problems. The doctor didn't feel I should have even attempted that pregnancy."

Pregnant? Danny thought. But if she was pregnant—this only confused her further.

"I was representing a couple who wanted to adopt a baby," Harris said. "After years of being on an adoption agency's waiting list, they gave up and came to me seeking a private adoption."

"You represented Jennifer?" Danny asked. Her mother was pregnant at the same time Jennifer had been pregnant. Her father was handling the adoption of Jennifer's baby, of *her.* So how had they ended up adopting her, and what had happened to the baby Millie was carrying?

He shook his head. "I represented the couple," he told her. "Another attorney represented Jennifer. I never even met her, never knew her name."

"How—" Danny began.

"I went into the hospital—there were complications." There were tears in Millie's eyes as she spoke. "The baby came, but was stillborn."

Stillborn. Their baby had died. But what about the couple who'd planned to adopt *her?*

"She was so depressed she was unable to leave the hospital," Harris remembered. "I—the doctors...we were worried about her, about her state of mind."

"How do I figure into this if another couple was adopting me?" Danny asked, confused.

"I'm getting to that," he answered her. "About this time, the couple withdrew from the adoption. The wife discovered she had cancer and only a short time to live. I thought we should adopt you but wasn't sure how your mother would feel—until she saw you." He paused. "I flew to Maine to get you—"

"Maine?" Danny asked.

He nodded. "Jennifer had gone there to give birth. She had friends there or something," he said. "I didn't tell her attorney that my clients had backed out. I wanted to see how your mother reacted to you before I told him anything at all."

"I'll never forget the night your father came into my hospital room," Millie remembered. "He was carrying you in his arms. You were so very beautiful. I didn't want to hold you at first—my heart was breaking for the baby I'd lost. But he said, 'You need a baby and this little angel needs a mother. You two really should get together.' And he put you in my arms."

"How did you feel about that?" Danny asked.

"Ambivalent," Millie confessed. "I told myself I couldn't replace the child I'd lost. But when I held you, well, I realized I couldn't let you go. You were my baby, too."

Danny didn't respond, couldn't respond. At the moment, she didn't feel like she belonged anywhere.

Mitch stood at the window in his office, staring out at the New York skyline without really seeing it.

He was thinking about Danny.

He hadn't heard from her since they returned to New York. The last time he saw her, she was literally driving off into the night, headed for Troy.

He looked over at the file folder lying on his desk—the file that had been waiting for him when he and Danny returned from Chicago. It contained all the information he'd requested before they left. His assistant had received it while he was away and created a file.

He frowned. His sources had been thorough, as always. They had provided him with even more than he'd expected. There had indeed been an adoption—a private adoption, no agency—and all court records had been sealed. If his contacts hadn't been so good, he could never have gained access to them at all. Danny had been adopted by the Vines after another petition to adopt her had been withdrawn.

And Millie Vine had given birth about the same time Danny was born. That infant was stillborn. No wonder it had been so easy for the Vines to pass Danny off as their biological child.

He wondered how much of this Danny knew by now.

Had she confronted her parents? he wondered. Was she still in Troy? What was happening? Why hadn't he heard from her?

He was worried about her. He couldn't help being worried about her. That was, he was learning the hard way, one of the hazards of being in love.

It was more of a hazard of being in love with Danny Vine than it would have been with any other woman.

Taking only a moment to think it over, he picked up the phone and dialed Danny's studio. One of her assistants answered on the second ring. "Divine Studios."

"This is Mitch Newman," he identified himself. "Is Danny in?"

Be there, he was thinking. Be there, Danny, and be all right so I can stop worrying about you.

But she wasn't.

"No. Can I take a message?"

"Do you know when she will be in?" he asked.

"Sorry, no."

"Do you know where I can reach her?"

Could she still be in Troy? he wondered again. She'd promised to call him when she arrived at her parents' home, to let him know she'd arrived safely. She hadn't called. She had promised to call him, to let him know how things were going there. Again, she hadn't. She'd promised to let him know when she was coming home.

Had she failed to do that, too?

"No. She hasn't called in, and I haven't been able to track her down."

"I see." Mitch thought about it for a moment. "If you do hear from her, have her call me, will you?"

"Will do."

"She has my number."

"Yeah, I know."

He hung up slowly, considering where to call next. Her apartment? Her parents?

He tried her apartment first—and got her answering machine. "Danny, it's Mitch," he said, speaking quickly. "I'm worried about you. Call me when you get this, will you?"

Hanging up again, he debated whether or not to call her parents' home in Troy. She might still be there, but he wasn't sure how she'd react. Danny, normally so laid-back and self-assured, had come back from Chicago a loose cannon. She was moody, volatile—totally unpredictable.

That, he conceded, was understandable. Her world had just been ripped apart. Her own identity was no longer clear to her. Nothing was what she'd always believed it to be. Dealing with the new reality was going to take time.

I suppose I'd be mixed up, too, if I were in her place, he told himself. But then, I really would have been better off if my father had put me up for adoption.

He dialed information and requested the number, then placed a call to the Vine residence. A woman answered. "Hello?"

Her mother, he guessed. He'd hoped Danny would answer.

"Is this the Harris Vine residence?" he asked.

"Yes, it is." There was an odd note in her voice, giving Mitch's instincts the feeling something could be wrong.

"Is Danny Vine there?"

Hesitation. "Who's calling, please?" she inquired.

"Mitch Newman."

"The investigator she hired?" The woman's tone was unfriendly. Something was definitely not right, but he seriously doubted he was going to be able to get her to talk about it, no matter what he said or did. He could only hope Danny was there to fill him in.

"Yes," he answered. "Is she there?"

"No, Mr. Newman, she's not." Just what he didn't want to hear. Where are you, Danny? he wondered, growing panicky inside. Are you all right? Why haven't you called?

"Has she returned to Manhattan, then?" Please say yes!

"I assume she has, yes."

"I've been trying to reach her," he explained, even though he was pretty sure the woman on the other end couldn't care less. Acknowledging his feelings for Danny, his concern for her, had caused an emotional dam to burst within his soul. He poured out his feelings whether she wanted to hear them or not. "I'm worried about her."

"I'm her mother, Mr. Newman," she finally identified herself, her tone softening a bit, "and I'm worried about her, too."

And she hung up on him.

Danny was alone in her apartment. The blinds were closed, the lights out—even the TV was off. She hadn't eaten, hadn't slept, hadn't showered. Her hair was a mess and she didn't care. She hadn't returned any of her telephone messages or opened her mail. She was huddled in her bed with the blankets pulled up around her like a cocoon. She wasn't sure how long she'd been holed up in her apartment. She only knew that she hadn't left it since she came back from Troy. Her parents had been open and honest with her, but they had not succeeded in softening the blow for her. This had been a shock for her. Never, in all those years when she was growing up, had she ever suspected the truth. Not even once. Didn't most adopted kids suspect? Even kids who weren't adopted suspected at one time or another.

I never had a clue, she thought miserably. I never even suspected. Not even once, not for a moment.

They'd covered their tracks well. Even the other children—her brothers and sisters—never suspected. But then, why would they? Her mother had been pregnant, after all, and when she came home from the hospital, she came home with a baby. They would have had no reason to be suspicious.

They should have told me, she thought, trying to justify the anger she felt toward them now. They shouldn't have let me find out like this. They shouldn't have let me think I was their own child.

How could they do this to me? she asked. She'd never felt so betrayed.

She was hurt and angry and confused. She wasn't even sure who she was right now. Was she Danny Vine or was she the Capshaw heiress? Did it matter? Would it change her?

It's already changed me, she thought sadly, drawing the blankets up over her head.

She wished she'd never heard of Connor Capshaw. She wished he'd never come looking for her. She wished Jennifer had never told him about her. She wished she could turn back time.

She wished Connor Capshaw had left his money to charity. Wasn't that what Barbara Fordyce had told her would happen to it if she refused to accept her inheritance?

Her inheritance.

She felt like such a fraud. She wasn't really a Vine, but she didn't feel like a Capshaw, either. How could she? They were strangers to her, just names in a will, photographs in an old family album, and not even *her* family album.

But then, which family was really hers?

She didn't want it, didn't intend to accept it. It wasn't her birthright, no matter what her bloodlines might happen to be. The Capshaws weren't her family.

And yet she couldn't stop thinking about David Capshaw and Jennifer Scott. They'd given her life, yet they might as well have been from another planet. They were strangers in a bunch of photographs. She felt no real emotional connection to them.

Or did she?

More often than she cared to admit, she found herself thinking about them, wondering what they were like, what kind of relationship they'd had, what kind of parents they would have been.

I look like her, Danny thought. I look like Jennifer. Enough like her that she would have recognized me if she'd seen me.

She tried to imagine what that would have been like, coming face to face with Jennifer. Would she have told Danny the truth? Would Danny have believed her? Would they have even liked each other?

Had Jennifer ever seen her? she wondered now. She tried to think. Had she ever met Jennifer Scott?

This was ridiculous, she told herself. She wouldn't know it if she had. The only photographs she'd seen of Jennifer had been taken when she was in her early twenties. She would have been in her late forties when she died. Her appearance would have certainly changed. Definitely. Yes, Jennifer had had cancer. That would have taken its toll on her physically. She would have looked different, a lot different, than she had in those photographs.

I could have seen her and never known, she thought. I had no reason to suspect, no reason to be looking.

If only it could have stayed that way.

She flinched at the sound of the doorbell. Ignore whoever it is and they'll go away, Danny told herself. Nobody knows I'm back. Pretend I'm not home. They'll go away.

"Danny?"

Oh, no, it's Mitch! Her mind was racing. Stay quiet, don't make a sound. He will go away.

But he didn't.

He kept ringing the bell, kept calling out to her, as if he somehow knew she was there. Why doesn't he go away? she wondered irritably.

"Danny?"

She didn't respond.

"C'mon, Danny!" he called out. "I know you're in there!"

How? she wondered. How does he know?

"Danny, open up!" he shouted.

She didn't respond.

Finally, it seemed he had given up. The knocking stopped. So did the doorbell. He was no longer calling out to her.

He's gone, she thought, relieved.

Then she heard the key turning in the lock.

Chapter Eleven

"Danny!" Mitch called out as the door opened before him. When he first arrived, before he went to get the super, he was certain he'd heard footsteps, the sound of someone moving around in the apartment. She had to be here.

No answer.

"Danny!"

Still no answer.

The building super, a short, balding man with a short, bushy mustache and protruding gut, followed him into the apartment. "You sure she's even here?" he asked dubiously, looking around the apparently undisturbed living room.

Mitch nodded. "Pretty sure, yeah," he said, checking out the kitchen.

No sign of life here, either, he thought, puzzled. The place was spotless, as if she'd cleaned everything top to bottom, then went off on vacation. It didn't make sense. He was sure she was here—or at the very least had been here.

"Before I came to get you, I heard someone moving around in here." Something's wrong, he thought, alarmed. Something is very wrong here.

"You sure it's her?" The super looked unconvinced. "I'm here all the time, and I haven't seen her since last week."

"Unless somebody else has a key to this apartment." Stopping to check the bathroom, he found it to be spotless, as well, as if it hadn't been used in a while. It didn't add up. He headed for the bedroom.

There, he found her—in bed, curled up in a fetal position under a mountain of blankets. At first she didn't appear to be moving. He could feel his heart beating up in his throat; his mind was racing. Please let her be alive. Please let her be all right.

He pulled the blankets away and looked down at her. She was fully dressed, had probably been wearing the same clothes for days. Her hair, normally so beautiful, was a mess.

"Danny," he said softly. "What's happened to you?"

"Go away," she breathed, waving him off.

The super came to the doorway. "You want me to call 911?" he asked, concerned.

Mitch shook his head. "I think she's okay—physically, anyway," he said. "I'll call a doctor if she needs one."

The super grunted his approval and left the apartment.

Mitch knelt beside the bed and gently pushed Danny's hair back off her face. "I've been worried sick about you," he told her.

"Go away," she mumbled, refusing to look at him.

"Can't do that," he said, shaking his head. "Now come on and get up."

"Go away!" she repeated.

Ignoring her stubborn refusal to cooperate, he grabbed her hands and pulled her to her feet. "What's gotten into you?" he asked.

"The truth!" she shot back at him. "That's what's gotten into me, as you put it."

"It's not the end of the world," he told her as he led her, resisting all the way, to the bathroom.

"Trade places with me and see how you feel!" she hissed angrily.

"You'll get through this," he assured her, stroking her hair.

"Right now I'm not sure I can even get through the day," she said darkly.

She stood before him, looking as if she'd spent the past week sleeping in Central Park. "A shower and some food might be a good start," he told her.

She shook her head.

She seems ill, he thought, looking at her now. But her illness wasn't of a physical nature. The pain Danny felt was deep and it was emotional. This is hitting her harder than I expected it to, he decided. A lot harder.

On the one hand, Danny was extremely resilient, the kind of woman who seemed able to take everything in stride. On the other, she was also a deeply emotional woman, something only those closest to her were aware of.

That was the Danny who'd been so deeply wounded by this new reality.

That was the Danny Mitch was worried about.

"How long has it been since you've eaten?" he asked, considering what needed to be done next. She obviously hadn't eaten in a while.

She shrugged.

She wasn't just avoiding the issue. She really didn't know. He was sure of it.

"When did you get back from Troy?" he asked.

Again she shrugged.

"You have to eat," he said promptly.

"Not hungry," she said, shaking her head.

"You have to eat," he repeated firmly, heading for the kitchen. "Take a shower," he ordered. "The food will be ready by the time you are."

Danny hesitated for a moment, then obediently went into the bathroom to shower. Mitch listened for a moment to make sure she really was in the shower before proceeding to the kitchen.

In her refrigerator, he found a dozen eggs, three kinds of cheese, sausage, butter and orange juice. There was a partial loaf of bread in the bread box. Enough—more than enough—for a decent omelet, he concluded. Just what the doctor ordered, something light but tasty and easy to make.

He immediately went to work.

When he was finished, he went back into the bedroom to get her. She was back in bed, pretending to be asleep.

At least she'd showered and changed clothes. That was a start.

Now to get her into the kitchen.

"Nice try," he said, pulling the blankets off her, "but it's not going to work. C'mon, breakfast is ready." He pulled her to her feet, then led her into the kitchen. Everything was on the table.

"I told you, I'm not hungry," she said stubbornly as he sat her down.

"You'll eat," he said, seating himself, "if I have to feed it to you."

Her eyes widened a little. "You wouldn't."

"Try me." He was fully prepared to force feed her if necessary.

She must have known he meant it, because she made herself eat—slowly, taking small bites, but eating nonetheless. Mitch watched her, relieved to see her eat anything at all. He poured her a glass of orange juice and buttered her toast.

"Better?"

Danny frowned. "Hardly."

"This isn't like you, Danny," he pointed out, taking a forkful. The cheese was gooey, just like the topping on a pizza. Just the way she likes it, he thought, remembering a breakfast they'd shared in Chicago.

"How do you know what is or isn't like me?" she challenged. "*I* don't even know. *I'm* not even sure who I am."

"You're Danny Vine, just as you've always been," he maintained. There were times his patience with her wore thin. He had to remind himself that this had been an incredible shock for her. She'd adjust.

If she made the effort.

"Am I?" she asked. "Or am I— Do you realize Jennifer never gave me a name?"

That obviously bothered her. She was confused and had not yet realized that the identity she already had was the only one she needed.

He managed a smile. "You have a name," he said gently.

"I know that," she acknowledged with a nod. "But with all that's happened—"

Reaching across the table, he covered her hand with his own. "With all that's happened, you're still Danny, you're still the same person," he stressed. "There's a new aspect to your reality, that's all."

Danny frowned, concentrating on her plate. "A pretty big aspect, don't you think?" she asked, taking a bite.

Mitch paused to sip his orange juice. "Only if you allow it to be."

"How can I *not* allow it to be?" she lamented, chewing thoughtfully. She took a bite of her toast, seeming to consider it further. "This was a shock. I was totally blindsided by it."

"That doesn't mean you have to let it derail your life," he told her. "Look at me."

"What about you?" she asked, regarding him with open puzzlement.

"I was a miserable kid," he reminded her. "My mother had died and I had a father who virtually ignored me."

"But you knew who your father was," she pointed out, reaching for one of the packets of mixed-fruit jelly she was always picking up in restaurants, because for some unfathomable reason they weren't sold in stores.

"And wished I didn't." The understatement of the year. His father wouldn't exactly win any awards.

She studied him for a moment. "What's your point?" she wanted to know.

"You've had a good life, haven't you?" he asked, trying to remind her of the life she'd had before all of this happened, the life she herself had told him was so wonderful.

"Well, yes."

"You had good parents, didn't you?" She was always telling him what wonderful parents she'd had.

"Of course!" she responded indignantly.

"Then why does it matter who gave birth to you?" he asked. "It shouldn't matter. It wouldn't have mattered to me if I'd had someone who really cared."

"It doesn't!"

"Then why are you tormenting yourself like this?" he questioned.

She gave a heavy sigh, pushing her hair back, away from her face. "I don't know," she admitted hesitantly. "I guess I was just reeling from the shock." She took a drink and reached for another slice of toast.

He smiled. She was hungrier than she'd been willing to admit. "Probably," he agreed, taking a bite.

"I've been acting pretty stupid, haven't I?" she asked. She poured herself more orange juice.

"I wouldn't say stupid," he said, shaking his head. Stubborn, maybe, but not stupid.

She grimaced. "I would."

"Don't be too hard on yourself," he cautioned.

Danny was silent for a moment. "I came down pretty hard on Mom and Dad," she remembered regretfully.

"What kind of explanation did they give for not telling you?" he asked, more than a little curious.

She took another bite. "Mom was pregnant," she began. "They knew it was going to be their last child."

"What happened?" His interest was genuine.

"There were complications," she said quietly. "The baby was stillborn."

"So they adopted you?" He got up to pop more bread into the toaster.

"There's more to it than that," she told him. "Mom was severely depressed. The doctors, they said, were concerned."

"How did—" he began.

She raised a hand to silence him. "My father was a lawyer then," she said. "He was representing a couple seeking a private adoption. But about the time the baby was born, about the time I was born, the couple had to back out."

"Why?" He sat down again.

"The woman found out she had cancer. She was dying." Danny frowned. "So there I was, a new-born baby without a home." The look on her face was one of deep sadness for the infant she had been, an infant who had been dangerously close to ending up homeless.

"Obviously not," he pointed out.

She shook her head. "Not for long," she conceded. "Mom needed a baby and I needed a mother. Dad decided we needed each other."

"Apparently he was right."

Danny nodded. "I guess I helped pull her out of her depression," she said as she finished the last of her omelet. "Anyway, when they decided to adopt me, they also decided not to tell anyone what had happened."

"No wonder no one knew you were adopted."
Mitch poured himself another glass of orange juice.
Under the circumstances, it had been easy for the
Vines to pass Danny off as their child.

She nodded. "Not even my sisters and brothers
were told," she said.

"That explains a lot."

"It explains why we were all clueless," she said,
nodding.

"And why I wasn't able to find a birth certificate," he said. There had to be a birth certificate
somewhere. And if there was an adoption, there had
to be a birth certificate *and* a record of the adoption
somewhere. He'd helped enough adoptees find their
biological parents to know.

"I was born in Maine," she said. "The birth certificate was, for lack of a better word, arranged."

"Even Franklin Ewing and Barbara Fordyce
didn't know that part," he recalled. Not so surprising, actually. Jennifer probably hadn't told Connor
Capshaw where the baby was born.

"Apparently Jennifer didn't mention it in her letter." Danny thought about it for a moment. "But if
they didn't know, how did they find me?"

"Easy," he said. "The adoption was finalized in
the state of New York." That was how it worked.
He'd done it himself many times.

"Where Jennifer was living at the time of her
death," Danny finished.

"Exactly."

"I should have realized."

"How did you leave things with your parents?" Mitch asked then, concerned that she was still at odds with them.

"Not good," she said with regret in her voice. "I was really shook up over it, and nothing they said or did seemed to make any difference."

"You're not going to leave it at that, are you?" he asked. She wouldn't have any inner peace if she didn't make peace with them.

She gave him a quizzical look.

"Don't you think you should go see them again?" he suggested. The sooner the better.

"I don't know—" she began.

"Make peace with them," he urged. "Don't wait too long." We have to put this behind us, he thought. We have to get on with our lives—our life together.

She thought about it. "You're right," she said finally. "You're absolutely right." Rising to her feet, she came around the table, bent down and kissed him.

Mitch realized now that he'd been waiting for this moment, waiting for it since Chicago—maybe longer. He pulled her down onto his lap and returned her kisses eagerly.

This was just the beginning...

They were definitely on the same wavelength, Mitch decided as he nuzzled her neck. He still found it hard to believe. He'd never thought he would ever find Ms. Right. He hadn't even thought he'd find

Ms. Maybe—but now, here he was with the most incredible woman he'd ever met. She was in his arms, wanting him just as much as he wanted her.

Loving him as much as he loved her.

"I do love you," he whispered, his declaration barely audible, muffled by her thick cloud of red hair. "I feel like I've waited all my life for you."

She was kissing his hair, running her fingers through it, her perfume intoxicating him. What was it—jasmine and rose? Yes...she liked to switch perfumes, to suit her mood, he thought. What was this one reflecting? What was it saying to him?

"I love you, Mitch," she murmured, running her hands down the length of his back. "Do you know how much?"

But before he could answer, the telephone rang.

"Don't answer it," he begged.

"Don't want to...but I have to." Reluctantly she withdrew and got off his lap. "If it's Phoebe and I don't answer, she'll come over here."

He let out a groan. "She knows you're home?"

"She always knows where I am. She has a weird kind of radar for things like that." She picked up the phone, spoke briefly, then hung up. When she turned back to Mitch, she had a pained look on her face.

"What's wrong?" he asked.

"It was Phoebe."

"And?"

"She's coming over anyway."

Chapter Twelve

The hot-air balloon was drawing a lot of attention.

A crowd had gathered in Central Park, where Danny was shooting for a beverage ad. The balloon was enormous and resembled a rainbow with its bands of red, yellow, blue, green, orange and purple. Its gondola looked, from a distance, like a gigantic wicker basket.

When Mitch arrived, he spotted Danny giving instructions to a team of assistants. He smiled to himself, thinking that she reminded him of a general shouting orders to the troops before going off into battle. One very attractive redheaded general—but a general nonetheless.

It's good to see her back to her old self again, he

thought, relieved. But then, Danny's resilient. It was a shock to her, sure, but I knew she'd bounce back.

Still, it hadn't stopped him from worrying about her. He'd never forget what had happened to her, to them. Neither of them would.

But it's all behind us now. We can't dwell on what's past, he told himself. We can only look to the future. Our future together.

He reached into the pocket of his leather jacket and fingered the small velvet box he was carrying there.

The ring.

He smiled to himself. The engagement ring he'd bought for Danny. Today he was going to ask her to marry him. He was going to persuade her to leave this three-ring circus with him and pop the question in a cozy little restaurant low on elegance but high on ambience.

Today, he would ask Danny to be his wife.

This was the most important moment of his life, and he wanted everything to be just right. He was determined this day was going to be perfect for both of them. It would be a day neither of them would ever forget.

She looked up and smiled as he approached. "Hey, good-lookin'!" she greeted him, smiling. "What brings you here?" She extended one arm to him.

"You do." They embraced and shared a brief kiss, then she withdrew, tapping his mouth with the tip of her index finger.

"Me?" she asked coyly.

"You," he repeated. "I came to take you away from all this."

She laughed. "Sounds tempting," she told him, "but no can do."

"I'm not taking no for an answer," he warned, pulling her close again.

"We don't have a choice," she said regretfully. "I'm already behind schedule." She gestured toward the balloon.

"You really can't leave? Not even for a little while?" He was unable to conceal the disappointment he felt.

She shook her head. " 'Fraid not. I wish I could." He could tell she was just as disappointed as he was.

"What about tonight?" he asked. Dinner would be good, he decided.

She thought about it. "Do you mind if it's late?" she asked somewhat hesitantly.

"Better late than never." More true than you know, he was thinking.

They were interrupted then by the loud, frantic shouts of her team of assistants.

"Danny!"

"Danny, come quick!"

"Where are Don and Eddie?"

"Get Danny!"

"The moorings came loose!"

"The balloon!"

"Look out!"

"The balloon's loose!"

"It's getting away!"

"Somebody stop it!"

"Quick—do something!"

"Where's Brian and Becky?"

"Who knows?"

"We don't need those two airheads!"

Danny gave an angry snort. "Great, just what I *don't* need!" Pulling away from Mitch, she broke into a run, pursuing the straying balloon.

"Wait!" Mitch ran after her. She really was crazy. And this was the woman he wanted to marry.

She didn't respond, didn't look back. She was moving as fast as her legs would carry her, trying to catch up to the balloon. Mitch wasn't far behind, but found it harder to keep up with her than he would have expected. Around them, everyone was shouting. As Danny caught up to the balloon, Mitch expected her to grab the ropes, to try to anchor it. She didn't. Instead, she leaped high into the air and vaulted, head first, into the gondola. The balloon began to pick up speed. Alarmed, he started to run faster, following her into the gondola.

She sat in the bottom of the gondola, her hair askew around her face, laughing. "I hope you know how to navigate this thing!" she gasped.

He laughed, too. "I was just about to ask you if you knew!"

They were oblivious to the crowd chasing the balloon, yelling as if that would somehow bring it back down. He pulled her to her feet and into his arms, and in that instant forgot all about his plans for a perfect, unforgettable evening. This, he thought, is as unforgettable as it gets.

This is it. Now or never.

"I love you, wild woman," he told her, laughing so hard that tears were streaming down his cheeks. "I've got to be out of my mind for asking, but will you marry me?"

She laughed, hugging him tightly. Her cheeks were streaked with tears, too. "You're right, cowboy, you are crazy," she said. "But now that you've opened your big mouth, you're stuck—you have to marry me!"

"Is that a yes?"

"You bet it is!"

They sealed the deal with another kiss.

"So how did they finally get you down?" Sally Vine wanted to know.

Danny laughed. "It wasn't all that difficult," she said. "We were never more than four feet off the ground."

"They just grabbed the ropes and pulled us down," Mitch confirmed with a nod.

The whole family had gathered that night at the Rainbow Room for a dinner party the Vines had thrown to celebrate Danny and Mitch's engagement. It was a formal affair, men in tuxedos and women in beaded gowns and jewels—except Danny. She wore a simple, ankle-length, sapphire blue gown, off the shoulder, with a beaded belt and little in the way of jewelry.

And ballet slippers.

The idea of a formal affair didn't appeal to either of them, really. Danny had objected to the idea of an engagement party since theirs was to be a short engagement. Within a few short days, their wedding would be followed by a reception. She felt two such celebrations so close together was too much. This, certainly, was too much.

But her mother had insisted.

Danny understood that her parents wanted to do something special for her and Mitch—especially now, especially after all that had happened. But they knew how she detested formal affairs, for heaven's sake!

"Danny?"

The sound of her sister Camille's voice cut through her thoughts. "Huh?"

"This was Mom's idea, wasn't it?"

"How'd you guess?"

"This isn't your cup of tea."

"You noticed."

"It must have been terribly romantic." This was Danny's sister Meryl.

"Of course it was romantic, silly!" her sister Karyn said. "He proposed there, didn't he?"

"Let me guess," Gene Vine began. "You were suffering from a lack of oxygen and didn't know what you were doing, right?"

Before Mitch could respond, and before Danny realized her brother's question hadn't been directed at her, they were joined by Harris and Millie.

"I wish you two would allow us to give you a real wedding," her father lamented, putting an arm around Danny's shoulders.

"Daddy, what we're having *is* a real wedding," Danny insisted. "It's just not a traditional wedding, that's all."

"What's wrong with traditional weddings?" her mother asked.

"Nothing, Mom." She sighed, rolling her eyes skyward. "It's just not for us, that's all."

Mitch grinned. "You have the world's most *un*-traditional daughter," he reminded them.

Millie frowned. "How well we know," she reluctantly admitted.

Danny kept smiling throughout the seemingly endless rounds of toasts and congratulations from friends and family, but as soon as the opportunity presented itself, she grabbed Mitch's arm and dragged him out of the restaurant.

"They're going to come looking for us, you know." He laughed as she dragged him into the elevator.

"Let them," she growled, drawing him close for a long, lingering kiss. "It'll be at least half an hour before anyone even realizes we're gone."

"We should've eloped," he muttered against her mouth.

"I agree. But it's a little late for that now," she pointed out.

"Is it?" He kissed her playfully.

"Yeah, it is. We've got a lot tied up in this wedding," she reminded him.

"That shouldn't bother you—you're an heiress now," he said, kissing her again.

"Get real!" she said, laughing and grabbing his tie. "You know I don't intend to spend any of that money!"

"On yourself," he clarified.

"On myself."

"Not even on the wedding?"

"Not even on the wedding."

"Or the honeymoon?"

"Or the honeymoon."

"What if I'm marrying you for your money!"

She poked his ribs. "You couldn't claim that. You care even less about money than I do!"

"You know me too well," he complained.

"I could say the same thing about you," she told him.

He kissed her again. "Have you decided not to tell them?" he asked then.

"My brothers and sisters? No, I'm not going to tell them—at least not yet," she said, her mood suddenly serious. "Maybe sometime, but not now."

"Do you think it would change things?" he asked.

"It might."

"You think they'll see you differently?"

"They might. I see myself differently," she confided.

"You're the same person you always were," he maintained.

"Maybe," she acknowledged with a nod, "but I went through life not knowing who I was."

"You know now."

She smiled again. "I know that in three days I'm going to be Danny Newman."

An identity she *could* be sure of.

It was a perfect day for a wedding. Clear and seventy-five degrees. The sun was shining, not a cloud in the sky.

There was, however, a rather brisk breeze.

Unfortunately.

Only Mitch seemed to welcome the breeze, and he wasn't saying why.

The wedding party gathered in Central Park early in the afternoon, seated in folding chairs, with the bride and groom standing under a canopy of wildflowers. The ceremony began promptly at 2:00 p.m., with vows written by the bride and groom. Mitch asked his grandfather to be his best man but did not invite his father or even inform Randall Newman he was getting married.

Danny asked all of her sisters to be bridesmaids. To avoid offending anyone, she had them draw straws to decide which of them would be her maid of honor. Sally won the draw.

The bridesmaids all wore print sundresses in peach, yellow and blue—no ugly, wear-'em-once bridesmaid dresses for her sisters, Danny had decreed—with wide-brimmed white straw hats. Danny also wore a white straw hat, though hers had a much wider brim than the others. Her dress was a pale peach silk, with a calf-length full skirt and sandals. Danny refused to wear high heels, even on her wedding day.

Mitch wore a white suit, as did his grandfather and Danny's brothers, who served as ushers. It was a double-ring ceremony, and the rings were wide gold bands engraved with their initials.

After the ceremony, a lavish reception was held at Tavern-on-the-Green. The wedding cake was three tiers and the main course of the dinner was Mitch's favorite, rack of lamb. This flamboyant restaurant, a fantasy of lights and antiques, seemed the perfect setting for the Vine-Newman reception.

"Where are you going on your honeymoon?" Nick asked.

Mitch laughed. "That's classified," he insisted. "Even Danny doesn't know."

Nick laughed, too. "How'd you ever keep it from her?"

"Wasn't easy," Mitch admitted. "You know how persistent she can be."

"Only too well!" Nick chuckled, rolling his eyes.

"I wouldn't call her persistent," Mike put in. "I'd call her nosy, pushy, bossy."

"Look who's talking!" Danny laughed, hooking her arm through Mitch's as she joined the conversation. "My brother—the pond scum at the bottom of the gene pool!"

"I've come up in the world—or down, as the case may be," Mike chortled. "I used to be just plain old pond scum."

"You'll always be some form of pond scum to me, big brother," she assured him, affectionately.

"So where's the honeymoon going to be?" Meryl asked as she approached.

"Ask him," Danny said, nodding toward Mitch.

"Sorry, that's a surprise," Mitch insisted.

Danny rolled her eyes. "I have this terrible feeling we're spending the next two weeks on Devil's Island," she said on a sigh.

"Not even close," he assured her.

The celebration continued until sunset. At that time, amid a shower of rose petals—rice was taboo since it was deadly to the birds in the park who might find it and eat it—Mitch and Danny left the restaurant in a hansom cab.

"Where are we going?" Danny asked.

"You'll see," he promised.

"Let me guess—we have a suite at the Plaza?"

"Nope."

"A helicopter ride around Manhattan?"

"Nope."

"What, then?"

"That."

She looked in the direction he was pointing. There, ahead of them, silhouetted by the fading daylight, was the hot-air balloon in which he'd proposed to her.

She looked at him. "This is a joke, right?"

He shook his head. "No joke."

"It's here for *us?*"

"That it is!"

Danny started to laugh. "Oh, no, what have you got in mind?"

"You'll see."

He jumped out of the carriage, then lifted her out. Hand in hand, they ran to the balloon and climbed into the gondola. As soon as they were aboard, their navigators took the balloon up. Before they knew it, they were high above Manhattan, heading out to sea.

A gust of wind blowing inland from the ocean snatched Danny's hat right off her head and sent it dancing across the sky, a thousand feet above the earth. Danny started to laugh.

"This is incredible!" Danny declared, hugging Mitch. "Absolutely incredible!"

"Just like you," he told her. Then he kissed her.

"I have a feeling I'm going to be very glad I married you," she said, kissing him again.

"I'm very happy to hear that," he said, "because I *know* I'm glad I married you!"

"Now," she began, kissing him again, "where *are* we going?"

"You're not going to give up, are you?"

"What do you think?"

"Okay," he surrendered. "Next stop—the Canary Islands!"

* * * * *

COMING NEXT MONTH

Conveniently Wed: Six wonderful stories about couples who say "I do"—and *then* fall in love!

#1162 DADDY DOWN THE AISLE—Donna Clayton
Fabulous Fathers
Jonas's young nephew was certainly a challenge for this new father figure. But an even bigger challenge was the lovely woman helping with the little tyke—the woman who had become this daddy's wife in name only.

#1163 FOR BETTER, FOR BABY—Sandra Steffen
Bundles of Joy
A night of passion with an irresistible bachelor left Kimberly expecting nothing—except a baby! The dad-to-be proposed a *convenient* marriage, but a marriage of love was better for baby—and Mom!

#1164 MAKE-BELIEVE BRIDE—Alaina Hawthorne
Amber was sure the man she loved didn't even know she existed—until the handsome executive made a startling proposal, to be his make-believe bride!

#1165 TEMPORARY HUSBAND—Val Whisenand
Wade's pretty ex-wife had amnesia—and forgot they were divorced! It was up to *him* to refresh her memory—but did he really want to?

#1166 UNDERCOVER HONEYMOON—Laura Anthony
Pretending to be Mrs. "Nick" Nickerson was just part of Michelle's undercover assignment at the Triple Fork ranch. But could she keep her "wifely" feelings for her handsome "husband" undercover, too?

#1167 THE MARRIAGE CONTRACT—Cathy Forsythe
Darci would marry—temporarily—if it meant keeping her family business. But living with her sexy cowboy of a groom made Darci wish their marriage contract was forever binding....

Take 4 bestselling love stories FREE

Plus get a FREE surprise gift!

Special Limited-time Offer

Mail to Silhouette Reader Service™

3010 Walden Avenue
P.O. Box 1867
Buffalo, N.Y. 14240-1867

YES! Please send me 4 free Silhouette Romance™ novels and my free surprise gift. Then send me 6 brand-new novels every month, which I will receive months before they appear in bookstores. Bill me at the low price of $2.67 each plus 25¢ delivery and applicable sales tax, if any.* That's the complete price and a savings of over 10% off the cover prices—quite a bargain! I understand that accepting the books and gift places me under no obligation ever to buy any books. I can always return a shipment and cancel at any time. Even if I never buy another book from Silhouette, the 4 free books and the surprise gift are mine to keep forever.

215 BPA A3UT

Name	(PLEASE PRINT)	
Address		Apt. No.
City	State	Zip

This offer is limited to one order per household and not valid to present Silhouette Romance™ subscribers. *Terms and prices are subject to change without notice. Sales tax applicable in N.Y.

USROM-698

©1990 Harlequin Enterprises Limited

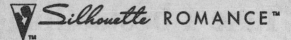

Silhouette ROMANCE™

is proud to present Carla Cassidy's
TWENTY-FIFTH book:

DADDY ON THE RUN
by
CARLA CASSIDY
(SR #1158, June)

Book four of her miniseries

Just when she was beginning to rebuild her life, Julianne Baker's husband, Sam, was back! He had left only to protect her and their little girl—but would Julianne be able to trust her husband's love again, and give their family a second chance at happiness?

The Baker Brood: Four siblings in search of justice find love along the way....

Don't miss the conclusion of **The Baker Brood** miniseries,
Daddy on the Run, available in June, only from

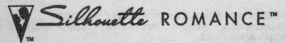

Silhouette ROMANCE™

BAKER4

SILHOUETTE® Desire® CELEBRATION 1000

is on its way in April, May and June 1996!

Join us for the celebration of Desire's 1000th book!
We'll have

- Book #1000, *Man of Ice* by Diana Palmer in May!
- Best-loved miniseries such as **Hawk's Way** by Joan Johnston, and **Daughters of Texas** by Annette Broadrick
- Fabulous new writers in our Debut author program, where you can collect <u>double</u> Pages and Privileges Proofs of Purchase

Plus you can enter our exciting Sweepstakes for a chance to win a beautiful piece of original Silhouette Desire cover art or one of many autographed Silhouette Desire books!

SILHOUETTE DESIRE'S CELEBRATION 1000
...because the best is yet to come!

DES1000TR

You're About to Become a *Privileged Woman*

Reap the rewards of fabulous free gifts and benefits with proofs-of-purchase from Silhouette and Harlequin books

Pages & Privileges™

It's our way of thanking you for buying our books at your favorite retail stores.

PROOF OF PURCHASE
Offer expires October 31, 1996
SR-PP148

Pages & Privileges ™

Harlequin and Silhouette— the most privileged readers in the world!

For more information about Harlequin and Silhouette's PAGES & PRIVILEGES program call the Pages & Privileges Benefits Desk: 1-503-794-2499

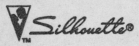

Silhouette®

SR-PP148